I0596441

ONE RED ARROW

PART I

BY CAITLYN GRABENSTEIN

Cover and Additional Illustrations by Drex

Map Illustration by JC Greening

Spiral Arrow Illustration by John Schieda

Umbravue Sketch by Caitlyn Grabenstein

This book was entirely crowdfunded.
Thank you all for believing in me.

A very special thank you to Nick, Brooks, Mom, Dad,
Bob, Amitai, Marie, Marsha, and Nicole

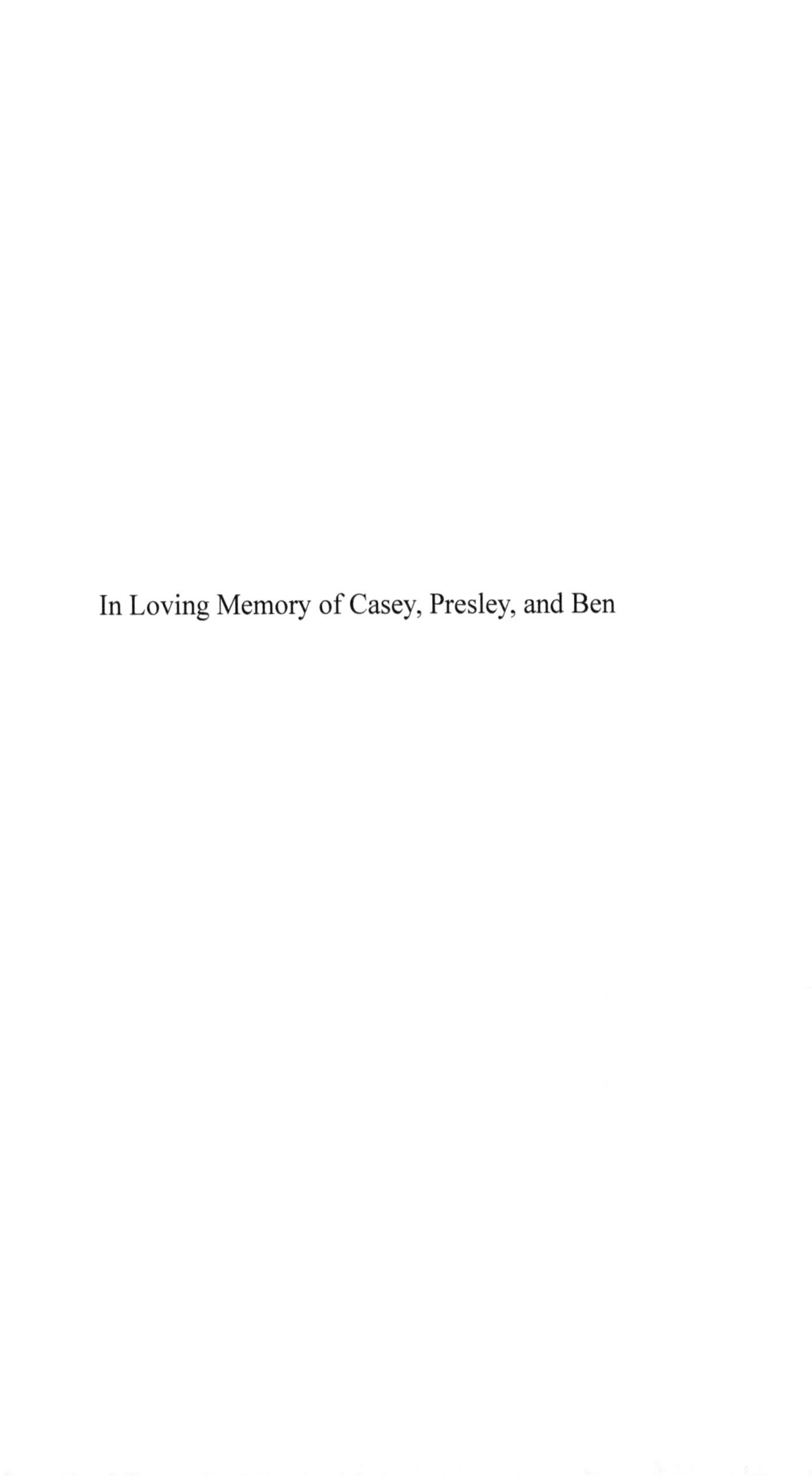

In Loving Memory of Casey, Presley, and Ben

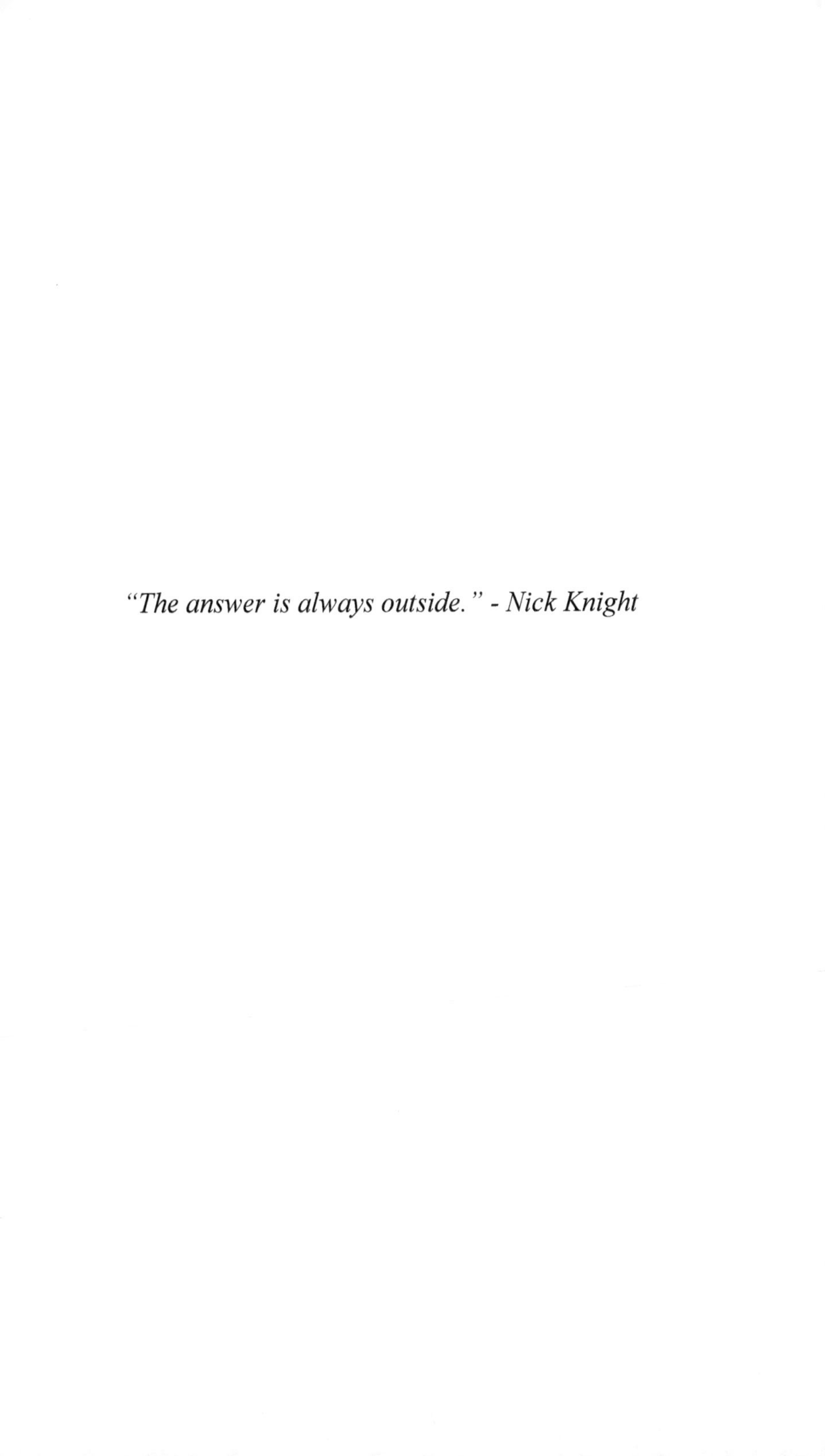

"The answer is always outside." - Nick Knight

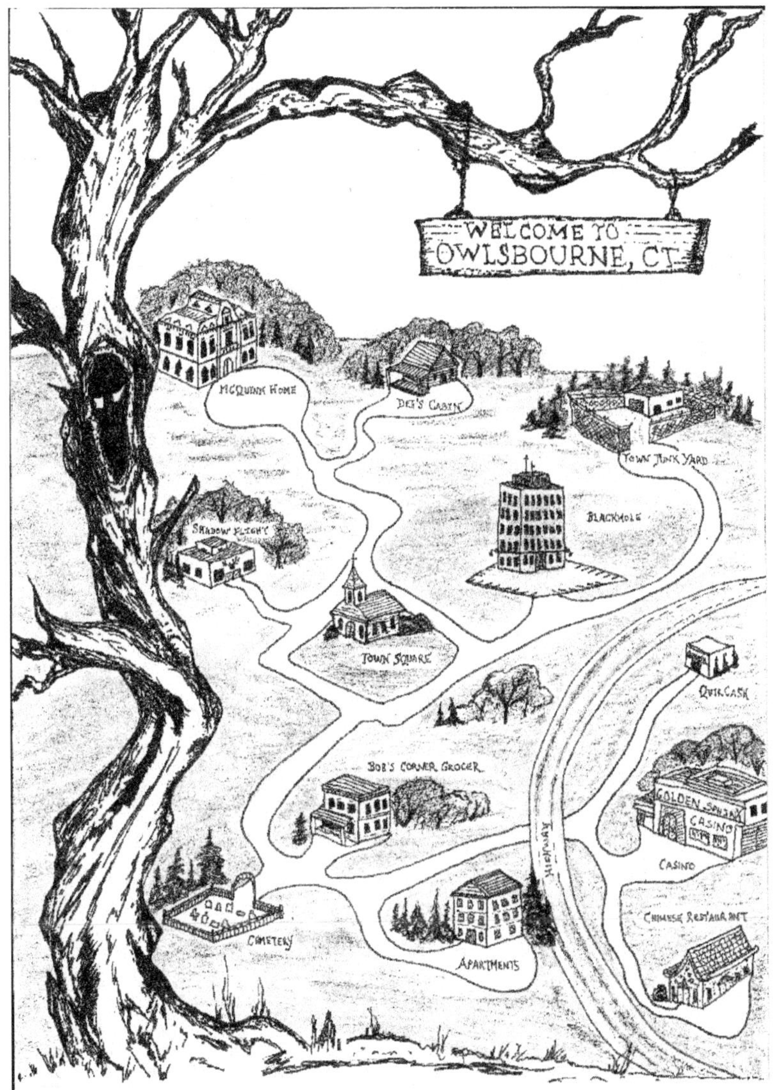

WELCOME TO OWLSBOURNE, CT.
McQuinn Home
Dee's Cabin
Town Junk Yard
Shadow Flight's
Blackmole
Town Square
QuikCash
Bob's Corner Grocer
Golden Spear Casino
Casino
Cemetery
Apartments
Chinese Restaurant

1989

The search party moved cautiously through the woods, careful to notice anything unusual. Stripped of their leaves, the trees stood tall and skeletal. It was a crisp November day. Fifteen people from town had volunteered their Friday afternoon to search for the missing hunter. They walked shoulder to shoulder, careful not to stray from the marked paths.

Sheriff Marcus Knight led the way, his eyes scanning every inch of the ground. Jonny Langley had been missing for seventy-two hours now, last seen heading into these woods with his rifle slung over his shoulder. The sheriff had known Jonny since they were kids; everyone in Owlsbourne had. Jonny was a staple in town. His jovial personality and kindness were what people dreamed about when they imagined small-town America.

"Keep an eye out for anything—tracks, clothing," Sheriff Knight called back to the group, his voice steady, though his face was tired and uneasy.

Even in daylight, the woods felt wrong. It wasn't just the usual late-autumn stillness; it was deeper, as if all the birds and animals had gone silent out of respect—or fear. The air was thick with the scent of damp earth and rotting leaves, and a mist clung to the ground, climbing up the searchers' ankles as they marched on.

"Sheriff Knight," someone whispered from the back.

Knight turned; it was Paulie, the butcher from town. Paulie had a nervous expression on his face. He clutched his flashlight in one hand, despite the sunlight. He was a tall man, but he seemed small here, dwarfed by the all-knowing oaks.

"What?" Knight whispered back, trying not to disturb the quiet. His own heartbeat pounded in his ears.

"Do you see anything? Isn't this all a little freaky? Like, why would Jonny disappear?" Paulie's eyes darted around the woods, as a nervous sweat poured over his eyebrows.

Knight couldn't help but follow Paulie's gaze. Every shadow stretched toward them, twisting into shapes his mind almost didn't recognize.

Sheriff Knight shook his head, trying to brush off Paulie's fear. He told himself it was just nerves—the cold air and the black coffee were tickling his brain, trying to counteract the three hours of sleep he'd gotten thanks to this situation.

The group came to a clearing, and everyone stopped. In the center of the clearing, lying in the underbrush, was the metallic sheen of a hunting rifle—or what used to be a hunting rifle. The metal of the barrel was melted into an unrecognizable pile of steel, flat and distorted.

Sheriff Knight knelt down to examine it as the townspeople gathered around him. A communal whisper rose from the crowd.

He examined the .270 Winchester rifle. He didn't touch it for fear of tampering with evidence. Still, he got close enough to notice that the walnut stock of the gun was charred black. He could barely make out the engraved initials beneath the flaky black wood. The initials read "JL." Knight had seen this rifle a million times in his life; it was Jonny Langley's gun.

"Jonny?" the sheriff called out, his voice louder, piercing the silence.

There was no answer—only the howl of the wind through the trees.

Someone stepped forward to look closer at the gun, but before they reached it, they froze, staring down at the ground directly below them. Sheriff Knight leaned in to see what had stopped them, and his stomach turned.

The earth around the rifle was muddy and disturbed, the dirt freshly churned.

"Everyone, back up!" Knight instructed.

Looking down at the ground, the townspeople took several steps back.

Leading away from where the remnants of the gun lay were tracks. They were unmistakably avian—but impossibly large. Each taloned imprint stretched over two feet long. Three forward claws splayed wide, while a backward claw left a deep stab in the dirt. Each print was gouged into the mud like the earth itself had been wounded.

The searchers followed the tracks with their eyes until the prints disappeared into the brush. The pattern was uneven, suggesting a hesitant shuffle—or perhaps a small hop— leaving behind an irregular path that vanished as abruptly as it had begun.

The landowner, Dee McQuinn, who was out helping the search party, gasped at the sight of the footprints, clasping a hand over her mouth. The hair on the back of Sheriff Knight's neck stood on end. He couldn't shake the feeling that they were being watched.

Before anyone could say anything, laughter arose from somewhere in the woods. The laugh was low, almost a chuckle—like someone trying to suppress a laugh, but too eager to keep it in.

Sheriff Knight felt a jolt of ice crawl down his spine.

The group looked toward the sound. The laugh grew louder.

"ha ha ha Ha Ha HA HA HA!"

Knight glanced over his shoulder, hoping to see someone— anyone—who might be playing a prank. But everyone around him looked as shaken as he felt, their faces pale and drawn.

The laughter stopped. A wave of dread washed over the crowd.

There, standing at the edge of the clearing, barely visible in the shadows, was a dark figure. It stared at the group with hollow, unfamiliar eyes. The figure wore tattered and dirty clothes. The being seemed disturbed—inhuman, even.

Knight froze. In that moment, he realized he was looking at Jonny Langley.

It would take the town thirty-five more years to find the first body—and by then, it would be too late.

Chapter 1

2024

FRIDAY

It just seems so easy for other people to live their lives, she thought to herself as the wind swayed the willow tree. Her treestand, ratchet-strapped against the trunk, gently rocked back and forth as her eyes fought to stay awake. Her compound bow hung unassumingly on a hook she had twisted into the bark next to her.

Two and a half hours, fifteen feet up in this tree, and no sign of life anywhere.

She shivered and wrapped her arms around herself.

For Kay McQuinn, just getting out of bed in the morning was an accomplishment these days. Existential dread brought on by the instability of her lonely life kept her in a chronic, negative thought spiral. She had built herself a mental prison of panic so strong the guys at Shawshank couldn't even dig out.

She knew life wasn't easy for everyone else, but recently, it sure felt like it was especially difficult for her. Panic attacks and compulsive rituals that had haunted Kay her entire life had crept into her days again.

A therapist told Kay years ago that not everyone thinks like she does. Not everyone feels dread for no real reason, has racing thoughts, catastrophizes, or obsesses.

Kay knew that was bullshit. Sure, not everyone was like her, but walk down any city street and you'll witness hundreds of people dealing with life in their own way: alcoholism, fanaticism, religion, fitness—whatever.

Kay had given up on therapy. She didn't love the idea of unloading the deepest parts of her life on a stranger. Plus, she didn't have an extra two hundred dollars per week to spare, now that her insurance didn't cover the sessions.

Being outside, sitting up in these trees, was as close to therapy as she would accept—and as close to God as she had ever felt.

Lost in a tired fog of thought, Kay noticed a red-tailed hawk land five yards away on a neighboring branch. Its eyes searched the ground for prey.

If she didn't get a deer this morning, at least she'd have this moment with the hawk.

Then, after only a few seconds, the hawk was gone—an exceptional predator, in and out, undetected.

Kay shivered and glanced down at her watch—7:05 a.m. Something should be moving now. She scanned the edge of the woods. Nothing.

Her breath made mini vapor clouds in front of her face. Her HotHands packets were starting to cool inside her fleece camo hand warmer. She had to climb down and head to work soon.

Come on, buck...

Over the years, Kay had invited friends and family to bowhunt with her, but they were always busy or uninterested. They didn't oppose hunting, but the idea of it "weirded them out." That's how her brother, Luke, described it one day, between bites of his Big Mac.

To Kay, ethically providing hormone-free, free-range meat to her family was one of her greatest accomplishments— especially with her bow and arrow. She couldn't stomach— literally—how animals were factory-farmed and treated these days.

Kay's grandmother, Dee McQuinn, had taught her how to hunt. Dee always said, "One red arrow can feed a whole village." All it took was one great shot to provide nourishment and life for so many people.

Kay missed Dee now, as she sat up in this tree. Dee had been her hunting partner and her best friend.

Her grandmother was beautiful. Kay remembered her with wild, silver hair that flowed down her back and over her shoulders. Her face was fine-lined and textured from decades of living in the wilderness. Her pale blue eyes held a quiet resilience and wisdom. She was in shape by any standards. Dee had endured all of life's challenges and showed Kay how to do the same.

Dee passed away a few years ago from pancreatic cancer. Life lacked color without her in the world to encourage Kay's passions and teach her about the woods.

The thought of Dee made Kay touch her bow. Her grandmother had given her the compound bow as a Christmas gift.

That special Christmas morning, snow flurried like in a Hallmark movie, as Dee and Kay stood side by side, shooting arrows at a practice target for hours. Dee's eyes were bright with pride. For a moment, the world had shrunk to only the two of them, standing in the stillness of the snow, bows in hand, smiling.

That was the last Christmas Kay remembered her grandmother being in good health. The next month, Dee was diagnosed with cancer.

This land had been her grandmother's property. Her grandmother had left it to her children, and right now, they were selling it. The sale was heartbreaking for Kay because she knew her grandmother's dream had been for the land to stay in the McQuinn family forever. Dee had always told Kay it would be a place for Kay to bring her children. But no one in the McQuinn family hunted anymore—except Kay. Come to think of it, most of them didn't even go outside very much. So Kay's parents, aunts, and uncles had decided this piece of property and its two-bedroom log cabin had to go. It had appreciated in value, and they could each receive a large inheritance from it.

Kay would buy the property if she could, but she didn't have the money right now, and her credit score was dismal.

7:20 a.m. – primetime. The sun was up, and the woods were coming alive. It was the first Friday of November, and the whitetail rut was in full swing. The freezing temperature that morning had the deer on their feet and moving around. Kay was sure she would see the big eight-point she had been tracking on trailcams for the last several months.

7:45 a.m. – still nothing…

8:00 a.m. – nothing. She was getting antsy because she knew she had to sneak down from the tree and go to work in a few minutes.

One more scan of the treeline with my binos, Kay thought.

Peering through the glass lenses, she moved slowly from left to right, analyzing every hint of movement, hoping to catch the flick of a white tail or the subtle motion of an antler.

Slowly…

She saw two large squirrels chasing each other up a broken limb and some chipmunks storing acorns in the hollow base of a maple tree. No deer yet, though the squirrels certainly sounded like a herd of deer bounding through the underbrush. Kay continued to scan.

Then, in a tangled window of branches, Kay spotted a large black silhouette perched on all fours up high—approximately sixteen feet up—in a pine tree. The creature wasn't just dark—its black skin devoured any surrounding light. Whatever it was, it was about one hundred yards from her location.

"What the heck…?" she blurted out, blowing her cover.

Kay couldn't get a look at the eyes, but the body was maybe seven feet tall if it stood upright.

The darn pines were so thick and difficult to see through.

She squinted. The creature's legs were lanky. The torso was tight and long. No hair, no extra fat. Its head looked egg-shaped and disproportionately large compared to the rest of its skinny, midnight-black body. She counted four bony, long fingers on each hand that resembled talons. The fingers wrapped around the branch. But they weren't clutching the branch—instead, they calmly held it, as if the creature were perfectly balanced and weightless. Whatever this thing was, it appeared to be defying the laws of gravity. It could have been a trick of the light or Kay's tired eyes, but for a moment, she thought she saw the creature's talon-like hands and feet lift off the branch just a little—as if it were floating.

A chill shot up the back of Kay's spine. A cool November breeze crept through the forest, and the subtle, unassuming evil of cold came with it. The woods shifted with the moving air, but the black creature stayed still.

Kay was frozen. Entranced. Terrified. She pressed the binoculars harder to her face, hoping—desperately—that her mind was playing tricks. But the closer she looked, the worse it got.

A thick, oppressive, early-morning fog clung to the creature's skin, wrapping around it like a hazy cloak.

The creature still wasn't looking at her.

Then its head turned.

Slowly, the creature's neck swiveled like an owl's, allowing its head to turn almost a full three hundred sixty degrees.

It moved like the red-tailed hawk—a predator on the hunt. Kay spotted a glint of a pulsing red glow on its chest.

There was an empty space where its mouth should have been.

The pines were still very thick, so Kay could only piece together quick glimpses of the silhouette.

Then the creature's giant, ominous, circular black eyes locked onto Kay with a cold, alien intelligence that made her stomach drop.

It was staring right at her. The creature blinked carefully and methodically with huge eyelids. It wasn't just looking at her—it was reading her, peeling away her thoughts like pages from a book.

She jumped in terror in her treestand, accidentally dropping her binoculars. Fortunately, the neck strap caught them.

"What the hell?"

Kay noticed now that the woods were quiet. No squirrels, no birds—not even the chirp of a cricket. Dead silence.

She grabbed her binos again. Kay wiped the sleep away from her eyes with the back of her hand. Blinked. And raised the binoculars back up to get another glimpse of the creature.

"Where's the branch? Where's the branch?" she mumbled, anxiously scanning the treeline. "There!"

Nothing. Whatever it was—it was gone. Vanished. No noise—not a crinkle of a leaf or a crack of a branch. Surely she would have heard something that large scurry down a tree.

Kay had been bowhunting for most of her life and trusted her senses enough to be sure that whatever that was, it wasn't right. She had to leave—and she had to leave now.

"What the fuck, what the fuck, what the fuck…"

Kay had forgotten about any big deer. All she wanted to do was get out of this tree and back to her car. She was awake now, eyes wide and stretched with horror.

Gathering her rattle antlers and grunt call, she unclipped her safety harness and scurried down the ladder one-handed, while clinging to her compound bow.

"Okay, okay… compose yourself," Kay said out loud as her feet hit the ground.

She was alone in these woods. No one was around to call for help. The immenseness of the forest became overwhelming.

"It's all good. You've been hunting these same sixty acres for twenty years—two-thirds of your life. You know these woods inside and out. Just get out of here," she said aloud to herself.

Kay fumbled with her gear and clumsily hurried toward the beaten-down walking trail. She'd have to run about a half mile back to her car.

Still, there was only silence in the woods.

So strange, she thought, as she picked up her pace.

The beat of her racing heart matched the slam of her pounding footsteps. Thank goodness the sun was up—this would be way freakier in the dark.

Crunch, crunch, crunch... Her boots announced her location with every step, like a beacon broadcasting, "Here I am!"

Stop sweating... get it together. Honestly, it was probably like a sick raccoon, she rationalized to herself, though she knew in her heart that wasn't true, as she barreled toward the safety of her car.

Her hunting gear bounced obnoxiously, and her heavyweight hunting clothes became even heavier than they already were.

You're super tired, and who knows... there are all kinds of animals in these woods. Get to the car. You have to be at work in thirty minutes, anyway.

Kay heard the sharp crack of a large branch behind her. Then another crack.

Followed by a heavy footstep. Then another.

Thud, thud, thud...

The steps reverberated through the forest, echoing each of her own.

Then, a faint, guttural humming sound surrounded her. The hum gradually grew louder. It was a strange, foreign sound—something not natural to the woods.

Kay was sprinting now. Sweat poured down her forehead. She was panic-stricken as she tried to get on top of her breath and her steps. Her chest was tight, squeezed by the cold, unforgiving fall air.

The hum reverberated in her ears. The familiar woods became a labyrinth of dread. Out of habit, she squeezed the silver wolf silhouette necklace dangling from her neck with her free hand. Kay dared not look back, though she sensed a presence closing in on her.

Her fingers reached for the fold-out skinning knife in her pocket.

Through the web of trees, Kay spotted Dee's cabin and her car in the gravel driveway. She wanted to slam the gas pedal and peel out of here.

"Just a little further!" Kay screamed to no one.

But when she finally glanced behind her—there was nothing.

The hum had stopped.

8:34 a.m. – Kay was back at her car.

Kay tore off her safety harness, binoculars, red wool hat, and mud boots and chucked them into the back of her '99 Jeep Cherokee with her bow.

The driver's side door whined open as she dove into the front. She locked the car doors.

Her anxiety was through the roof. Kay was familiar with panic attacks, and this encounter had sent her fight-or-flight response into overdrive. She was panicking.

She took a few deep breaths and cleared her head.

"It was an animal. No big deal. Maybe it was even a small black bear. There are a few of them still wandering around before winter," Kay told herself.

She couldn't bring herself to imagine what else she might have encountered.

She took another deep breath and rationalized further: "It was probably the freakin' Bennett boys' kids chasing you. Idiots."

The Bennetts were Dee's neighbors. Merle and Wade Bennett had grown up in Owlsbourne. They caused constant trouble growing up. They had been trespassing on Dee's land for decades.

The Bennett boys had inherited their family's compound— a cluster of trailers and broken-down trucks—on a fifty- acre plot in the middle of the woods. That's where they lived with their wives and grown children.

"Yeah... the Bennett boys—that was it," she breathed a sigh of relief. Though she didn't really believe it.

She turned the key, hit the gas, and sped out of the driveway.

Chapter 2

8:58 a.m. – "Hey, Kay! Can you get those designs to me by noon? I have a meeting with BlackHole at 1:00 p.m.!" Fred, Kay's boss, shouted at her as he walked out the door to his favorite coffee shop. He went on his extra-long breakfast run every morning like clockwork.

"You got it!" she called back to him.

Kay meandered through the stark, gray corporate lobby. She could smell the scent of industrial cleaner and tired ambition. "Fake Plastic Trees" by Radiohead blared through the single earbud she'd bothered to wear as she made her way to the elevators.

She couldn't stop thinking about the strange animal she had encountered in the woods. No way she was going to tell anyone about it. Everyone at work already thought she was weird for bowhunting—and just weird in general. All Kay wanted to do was put the creepy incident out of her mind. She had too much to focus on at work. She couldn't spend the day spiraling over what was probably a sick black bear with mange.

Alone in the elevator, Kay pulled at her shirt, ran her hand through her hair, and wiped some sweat from her brow, trying to remove any hints of the woods that still lingered before she got to her desk.

They'd really developed the town of Owlsbourne in the last several years, and now her grandmother's property was only a twenty-minute drive from dozens of modern industrial parks and bleak strip malls—including her work building.

The company she worked for, Mytherra, was in offices nestled between a hideously drab realty firm and a Smoothie Emporium. Boy, how her life had changed in the last five years.

Chapter 3

A few years earlier, Kay was a viral internet sensation; she was invited to do interviews with major news networks and had nationally known brands as regular clients. Her original art was a wonder to her adoring fans. Kay thought nothing special about her art; she'd been making some form of art her entire life.

Kay was self-taught not just in art, but in almost everything she wanted to accomplish. If Kay wanted to do it, she'd figure out how.

The visual art that she started making after college was different from her other projects, and its popularity took off like wildfire. Kay created surreal, colorful digital paintings of ideas or scenes that came to her mind.

Dee, her grandmother, was the one who encouraged Kay to share her surreal art with the world. Dee claimed Kay had a God-given gift. Kay didn't believe that, but she loved creating, and if she could make money doing it, then why not share it?

With Dee's persistent pushing, Kay started posting her art on PicsPost (a photo-sharing social media app), and that was that. Kay became an overnight viral success. Her art account inflated from twenty thousand followers to over one million followers in just four months. Of course, success like that never truly happens overnight.

Kay spent years working as a custodian, a waitress, a data entry clerk, an assistant, an exercise instructor, a janitor, and a dog walker while trying to get her art off the ground. She spent fifty to sixty hours per week working odd jobs, and the remaining time creating, alone in her apartment, with her dog, Shotgun, a forty-pound brindle hound mix.

When her original art started making a profit, Kay moved to Philadelphia. Philadelphia was a tremendous upgrade from the small farm town of Owlsbourne, Connecticut, where she was born and attended community college.

Kay excelled in Philadelphia. She made friends, attended fancy corporate events, was invited to highbrow luncheons with hypocrite artists and critics, and, honestly, grew a big head about the importance of her work. The internet has a unique ability to inflate an ego and then destroy it.

At twenty-six years old, Kay hired an assistant and felt above the life she was handed. To all the family and friends who told her she couldn't make it in the arts, look at her now.

Until BlackHole.

BlackHole Pharmaceuticals Inc. was the largest pharmaceutical company in the world. BlackHole Pharmaceuticals Inc. was also headquartered in Owlsbourne.

BlackHole was founded by Owlsbourne native, Siren Hex. Siren made Darth Vader look like a cuddly teddy bear.

Siren was a chemist by trade who built BlackHole from the ground up. She was smart, strategic, and about as sentimental as a knife.

Siren was in her fifties. Her brown hair was cut into a chin-length bob that never seemed out of place. Siren lived in pantsuits. She had high cheekbones, sharp features, and clear, smooth, porcelain skin. She was of medium height but had the kind of presence that made people straighten up when she walked by. Siren didn't wear much makeup, just enough to look polished, never fussy. Everything about her was intentional.

The only thing that ever made Siren look soft, in commercials or interviews, was her daughter, Veronica. Siren was a single mom, and while she rarely talked about it, the love was there, tucked quietly beneath all the sharp edges.

Siren founded BlackHole after her husband, Veronica's father, died from Huntington's disease.

BlackHole started as an affordable internet medication marketplace but quickly became the global leader in pharmaceuticals. BlackHole's market dominance soon loomed over most of the world, with its offices, warehouses, and employees in every major city.

Most of the residents of Owlsbourne worked for BlackHole.

People praised BlackHole for bringing jobs and wealth to a slowly dying farm town. Kay didn't quite see it that way. Kay saw the company for what it was: a dishonest, greedy corporate giant that crushed anyone who stood in its way— little did she know, eventually it would crush her too.

Chapter 4

One morning, while living in Philadelphia, Kay was walking to meet a new art client when she looked up and saw a giant billboard with her original art on it.

She hadn't sold that art piece to anyone.

The billboard displayed "BlackHole" in large, bold letters across the sunflower sky of her painting. Her art was being used to advertise a new seasonal allergy medication, Allerzil.

The only difference was that her art was changed ever so slightly. Kay later learned that BlackHole had done this to avoid any copyright infringement.

Kay was all too familiar with situations like this—sellers on various online marketplaces and repost accounts frequently attempted to steal her work, like they did with countless other artists.

But for such a massive corporation to steal so obviously? That was bold.

Most people suggested Kay let it all go: "There is no way you'll beat BlackHole's legal team. Just let them have the art. You can always create new art."

But it wasn't in Kay's nature to back down—not yet, anyway. BlackHole would change that. So, she leaned into a legal battle with BlackHole.

Kay's father, Dee's son, Bruce McQuinn, who worked for BlackHole, just like most everyone else in Owlsbourne, helped pay for Kay to hire an attorney.

The attorneys went back and forth for months. BlackHole claimed that the art was their original art because of the minor edits they had made. They refused to remove the ad because Allerzil was so successful, nor would they pay Kay what she deserved.

The advertisement ended up being the most popular BlackHole ad ever. Kay's art was everywhere—billboards, commercials, magazines, and even on the Allerzil bottles themselves.

In the end, those who discouraged Kay from taking legal action were right. Kay spent all the money she'd saved from new client work on legal fees but got nowhere.

As a last resort, Kay threatened to expose BlackHole's theft publicly. Through her attorney, she warned them she would share the truth with her million-plus followers: that BlackHole had stolen her art. She hadn't done this yet because she was still hopeful they would reach a fair settlement.

Instead of making things right, BlackHole responded with their own threat: BlackHole's Public Relations team would step in.

But why go to such lengths to silence her? Why not simply pay her what she was owed—or at least give her credit?

Kay refused to back down. It was her art, and she wouldn't let them take it without a fight. That was when the smear campaign began. Suddenly, she found herself at the center of a firestorm—canceled and her reputation in ruins.

Kay quickly came to understand the fleeting, shallow nature of adoration.

One morning, after the threat from BlackHole (which Kay stupidly assumed was an empty threat), she woke up to countless messages and comments berating her art—and her. One of her art pieces had gone viral.

The piece was a painting of a woman bowhunter hunting an elk on the moon.

A few anti-hunting groups got ahold of the image, and that was it. Kay's hard-earned reputation was diminished to less than nothing. The anti-hunting groups made her art into a viral poster for animal cruelty and abuse. With this new, horrible message, the art spread rapidly on social media.

Kay knew BlackHole's PR team was behind the anti-hunting messaging, the bot accounts, and even some troll accounts. The timing was not a coincidence—this was the smear campaign they had threatened.

Internet trolls not only ridiculed Kay's art, but they also found Kay's photo on the internet and started creating hateful videos, mocking and making fun of her as an artist and as a person. Kay became one of the most hated people on social media. The trolls degraded her art, nose, eyes, hair, voice, education, and life. Though they were your typical armchair critics who knew nothing about Kay's life, their words still stung like a wasp, mean and unrelenting.

Brands, businesses, and friends associated with Kay took a step back to avoid being caught in the crossfire.

Kay's intentions didn't matter. Of course, she never intended to promote animal cruelty with her art. Still, she was canceled. BlackHole had won—and so had her stubbornness. Why didn't she just let the Allerzil ad go? Why did she have to fight BlackHole?

Her livelihood and business were destroyed as the world, unaware, slowly ticked on.

Kay told herself that she could handle it. She blocked the trolls and kept on creating. But the comments and hate kept coming.

She couldn't ignore it all. The comments dug deep under her skin, leaching off her bones, preying on her insecurities. She built anxieties that she didn't even know existed. Kay didn't want to walk Shotgun or leave her apartment. She couldn't look at photos of herself. Her life felt distant and not her own. Kay thought about killing herself every day, like the trolls on the internet had suggested.

Panic attacks she had experienced earlier in her life returned with vicious vengeance. What Dee claimed was

Kay's gift—Kay's visual thinking and expansive imagination—turned into her curse.

During that time, her obsessive-compulsive disorder became a cruel, relentless bully. Constantly sabotaging Kay's mind with unwanted thoughts. She had OCD—and not the popularly misunderstood version of OCD where a person just cleans a lot. This was dark, true OCD that consisted of paralyzing, grim, intrusive, visual thoughts. The thoughts were crippling and invasive. Kay became attached to the idea that she could never operate like a regular person again.

Kay never talked about her diagnosis. Her own mental warfare was a daily battle. She white-knuckled her way through most of her days. She had found art to be a coping mechanism for her OCD and subsequent depression, but now that coping mechanism was shattered—it was dirty and tainted.

Kay was in the dark. She had fought the dark in small bits her whole life, but now she was fully immersed, drowning for months. The weight of the hatred, shame, and judgment made her feel like the entire sky might collapse at any moment and crush her. Gravity became her enemy. She would have panic episodes where she was positive that she would fall off the face of the Earth. Her body would shake uncontrollably, her mind would spin out of control, and tears would stream down her cheeks as she hugged Shotgun.

Kay slept longer, ate almost nothing, created less, and lost more clients because of the bad press.

Any money she had left leaked out of her bank account.

The friends that she had made in Philadelphia, while she was successful, all disappeared the moment she didn't have clout to offer them. Kay learned the hard way that some people would sacrifice years of a relationship in defense of complete strangers if it meant that, ultimately, they could get ahead.

Kay didn't call her family; she didn't need their opinions, and she didn't rely on friends. She saw a therapist for a few weeks. Maybe that helped. Maybe she just needed someone to talk to. She was a private person, and, most importantly, she was embarrassed about being so shaken by bullies.

Kay reluctantly started taking a combination of Celexa and Xanax, a duo that she had been prescribed a few times throughout her life for her OCD and depression. Of course, Kay's measly insurance only covered the generic BlackHole-brand of her medications, adding salt to the wound.

The instant relief of medication was stark. The drugs made her feel like a zombie; she didn't cry anymore; she didn't really laugh either, but the drugs tempered the panic enough for her to exist with less pain.

Kay hated BlackHole.

It was all so on-the-nose—an evil corporate company with a shady CEO and a growing global empire—it was every comic book trope rolled into one. Too bad it wasn't fiction.

Poor and finally broken, Kay moved back to her hometown of Owlsbourne and rented a room from a local chef for a quarter of her rent in Philly. The room in East Owlsbourne was all she could afford. The chef was an older, kind gentleman named Carlo. He was six foot two inches with thinning gray hair, blurry black tattoos, a crooked, yellow smile, and a potbelly. He watched his true crime shows late at night while downing a six-pack of PBR and smoking Marlboro Reds. Every once in a while, Kay would join him for a cigarette and a beer, and he'd tell her all about his wild life in Texas before "he settled down." He was nice to Shotgun and made meals for him and Kay when he wasn't cooking in the restaurant.

Kay's family thought she was crazy. First, they thought she was crazy for ever pursuing art at all. "That is not a career for a respectable woman," her mother, Pam, would preach. Then, once she failed, they thought she was nuts for renting the room from Carlo. Still, anything was better than taking a handout from the McQuinns in the form of money or somewhere to live. Kay didn't want to live with her parents and constantly hear about how she should have pursued a law degree, like her sister. Then again, maybe they had a point… maybe then she could have beaten BlackHole's legal team.

However, thinking she was nuts and discouraging her when she was trying to make it did not stop her family from bragging about Kay's art accomplishments to friends and colleagues when she succeeded.

Once back in Owlsbourne, Kay weaned herself off the prescription medication she was still relying on and started trying to face her demons head-on—*that* she was proud of.

Chapter 5

All those events brought her to the elevator at Mytherra on this wintry November morning, heading to her beige, fabric-walled cubicle where she would wait to clock out for her thirty-minute lunch.

She spent her days typing prompts into a machine. The "designs" her boss, Fred, was referring to were AI art of words that Kay inputted into a computer program.

Kay went from days full of imagination and art to days of computerized sketches and thirty-minute brown-bagged lunches. Yes, she felt defeated. She felt like a caged animal. Kay would be ashamed if her grandmother, Dee, saw her like this now, giving up and moving through each day like a wandering corpse.

To Kay, there were only two kinds of people in this world: people who gave up and people who didn't. She didn't want to give up, but she didn't know how the hell to move forward, either. Or maybe she knew how to move forward but didn't want to. Maybe she had grown to love the complacency and unaccountability of this soft, mundane life. Kay always felt more comfortable in failure than in success, and to her, this job, this existence, this unhappiness certainly felt like failure.

Nature never gave up—that's why Kay loved it so much. That's also why she was so ashamed of herself for working at Mytherra and not making art anymore.

Kay stared at herself in the streaky office bathroom mirror. The stark overhead light flickered as she brushed her jagged bangs out of her eyes. Her Italian heritage gave her healthy, untamed hair that was cut into a long, '80s-style shag. She had olive skin and sharp features—features only softened by her dad's Irish and English blood. She stood around five foot five inches, not super skinny, but not obese. "Just average," she said out loud, looking at her own pale blue eyes. Her eyes were her "best feature," her mom had told her many times when she was young. Right now, those eyes welled with tears.

Kay used to run every day. She loved exercise. Now, her version of exercise was dragging herself off the couch to grab the delivery food left outside her apartment door.

Kay pulled out her phone and scrolled through PicsPost. She had left her art account untouched since BlackHole stole her art, but she stayed logged in. It all hurt so much. Kay had unread messages from celebrities and fans. She just didn't care anymore. None of the superficial glitz mattered.

Kay had met a lot of her heroes; she'd gone out and lived her life to the fullest, and ultimately, she met the wizard behind the curtain. She learned what made a lot of the world tick: money, vanity, and greed. Kay was a cynic. She often wondered how many other curtains existed in her reality.

She used a wet, cheap, brown paper towel to wipe some spilled black coffee off her Joni Mitchell T-shirt. Then, she tucked the silver wolf necklace under her shirt collar and pulled her right sleeve over the tattoo she had on her bicep of a trout biting a hook. Kay bent down and tightened the hanging laces on her worn-out combat boots. She glanced back up at the mirror, stared at herself, took a breath, and walked back to her cubicle.

Kay grabbed the prints of the designs off her desk for Fred and hopped on the elevator to his office.

His office was in the back corner of the top floor. He had a panoramic view of Owlsbourne.

She knocked.

"Come in!"

"Oh, hi, Kay! You're a lifesaver, you know that?" He snatched the designs from her hands. "BlackHole is going to love these!" as he rifled through the pages.
"You're my secret weapon." He winked at her.

"Yuck," she thought. By secret, he meant he took credit for all of her work; he took credit for most people's work.

A photo of Fred and his family sat on his desk. In the picture, he had his buff arms around his two kids and wife, his greasy forehead gleaming in the sun, his beady black eyes hidden behind Gucci sunglasses. His new salt-and-pepper hair plugs and freshly whitened veneers made him look… good. If Fred weren't creepy, he'd be kind of attractive. But his smile was just a little too wide, and when he looked, his eyes lingered too long.

He once told Kay that she looked just like his wife, which was totally inappropriate. He was well known for making bizarre and, frankly, gross comments to the women in the office.

"I'm happy you like them," Kay answered as she backpedaled toward the door.

"Let's have a working lunch sometime, Kay! I can mentor you so that you aren't stuck doing grunt work forever," Fred offered. "You know, your art had a lot of potential."

"Yeah, maybe! Thanks!"

Without another word, Kay made a beeline for the elevator.

12:14 p.m. – Pre-packaged dollar store deli turkey and yellow mustard squished between two slices of stale wheat bread. Kay took a bite.

"So, what I was saying was that I know I'm going to be a millionaire," Harold continued, while crunching on salt and vinegar chips, as he and Kay finished their lunches in the breakroom.

Harold was Kay's coworker and probably the closest thing she had to a friend. He always talked about his business ventures that were "going to take off." Today, Harold was exploring the idea of starting a new television streaming app he called TimelessTelly.

"I'm telling you! This is it! Exclusively vintage television shows in your pocket all the time!"

It actually sounded like a decent idea, one of the cooler concepts he'd come up with. The issue was that Harold enjoyed talking much more than he enjoyed doing. So, Kay tuned out his rambling most of the time. He was an IT expert by trade and a nice guy. He was fascinated by Kay's bowhunting stories. His wife, Florence, made some killer chocolate chip cookies. When he wasn't talking about his big future plans, he was talking about Florence. He was smitten with her, even after six years of marriage. Florence stayed home with their three-year-old son, Scout, while Harold brought home the bacon.

Harold slouched in his chair; his bony shoulders curled in to protect his tiny body. His wire-rimmed glasses slid down his wide nose. Potato chip crumbs littered the front of his horizontally striped polo shirt. Harold's pale blond hair hung loose on his head, swinging from side to side as he excitedly talked about TimelessTelly. He wasn't young, but he wasn't old. Kay guessed he was a few years older than her. Come to think of it, he had never volunteered his age, and she had never asked.

"Man, I wish you had kept your PicsPost account active! You'd probably be like a legit celebrity by now! Do you think you can show me how to market TimelessTelly on social media? You're a pro. Maybe you can make the art for my business!"

Kay just nodded. Harold would be onto his next big idea in a week or so.

She was distracted. She couldn't stop thinking about the animal she had seen in the tree earlier. Was it an animal or creature of some sort?

Kay knew all the cryptid stories about Mothman, Bigfoot, the Rake, etc. Her late nights, not sleeping, were spent mindlessly staring at new, "real" paranormal shows on TV. She was interested in that stuff, but not a believer; it was all just kind of intriguing to her.

Could the animal have been a cryptid? No way. It was probably a baby black bear with mange or a deformity or something…

For a moment, she had a faint memory of Jonny Langley. Didn't something strange happen to him years ago on Dee's property? Like in the '80s? Still, Kay distinctly remembered that the Bennett boys had taken credit for that incident. It all turned out to be a big prank. They were thrilled because they were featured on the local evening news.

"Are you in?" Harold asked.

Kay snapped to reality. "I'm sorry, what?"

"Do you want to come to game night tonight with Florence and some of our friends? It's Catan night!" He was almost begging.

"I wish I could, but I have dinner with my family. My brother is in town visiting."

"Ugh… okay… well, we have game night every Friday night. So, maybe next week! We really want you to come!"

Harold really was a nice guy.

"Thank you for the invitation. I'll be there soon!"

No, she wouldn't be. She had little interest in small talk with strangers over a board game that would take her hours to understand. Plus, most of her conversations with people, lately, resulted in them asking her for art or marketing tips. It's weird how you age and how your value becomes a bartering tool for people. A lot of exchanges in adult life are unspoken transactions.

She knew not everyone wanted something from her. But, with the marginal success that she once had, she learned that she could only ever trust a handful of people, and she could only ever fully trust herself. That was another motto that Dee always preached: "Trust yourself, Kay. You are all you have."

Harold's friends were probably nice. But Kay was a loner, a solitary person, and she liked it that way.

"Fine, fine. Well, Florence can't wait to catch up with you at the Bicentennial on Monday night!" Harold pressed. The Owlsbourne Bicentennial Celebration would be held at the town green in a few days. The event was sponsored by BlackHole. Kay felt obligated to go because all her coworkers and family planned to attend.

"I look forward to catching up with her too!" Kay responded, trying to hide her disinterest, as she got up to head back to her desk and watch the minutes tick by for the rest of the long afternoon.

Chapter 6

5:02 p.m. – It was a fifteen-minute drive through windy, backcountry roads to Kay's parents' house on the edge of Owlsbourne. Her parents bought a monstrous, newly built home with a heated pool (they never failed to mention that) after her father's promotion to Vice President at BlackHole.

Kay couldn't blame him for working at BlackHole; he had worked there long before her battle with the company, and these days, it seemed like everyone worked for BlackHole. She understood he had a mortgage and bills to pay and couldn't just leave his job, in solidarity or protest.

She clocked out of work at exactly 5 p.m. Dinner was at 6:30 p.m. That gave her an hour to hang out at her favorite archery shop, which coincidentally was on the way to her parents' house.

Shadowflight Archery was nestled in the woods of Owlsbourne. Dee took Kay there for the first time when Kay was five years old, and Kay had been going regularly ever since.

Kay's forest green Jeep Cherokee squeaked into the parking lot as the sun set over the flickering neon "OPEN" sign. The green roof of the lodge-style store blended into the surrounding trees. Seeing this building always made her heart warm. Shadowflight was Kay's church; it was her place of congregation, positivity, and happiness.

"How are you, Kay?" Nick, Shadowflight's best employee, greeted her as she walked into the log building.

"I'm good! Same ol', same ol'," she answered distantly. She couldn't stop thinking about that black creature from earlier.

Kay studied a package of expandable broadheads on the shelf.

Jimmy walked by. Jimmy owned Shadowflight Archery and was one of the nicest, calmest people Kay had ever met. He was a stocky, heavier guy in his late forties. He always kept his hair cut short, in a crew cut, and he had a kind smile that never left his face, revealing gentle crow's-feet at the corners of his eyes. Jimmy was the all-American dad. He knew Kay's family and watched Kay grow up over the years. From organizing block parties to coaching Little League, Jimmy's larger-than-life personality had earned him a special place in the hearts of the citizens of Owlsbourne.

"Hi, Kay!" Jimmy greeted her warmly as he passed by with another customer.

"Hi, Jimmy! The store looks great," Kay complimented.

"Thank you so much!" Jimmy smiled. "Tell your dad that I said hello. We miss seeing him around here."

"I will!" Jimmy nodded and walked off.

Kay turned back to the broadheads. "What do you think of these expandables?" Kay questioned Nick.

"They're supposed to be great. Everyone who comes in here loves them. But, between you and me, I don't trust them. What if they malfunction when they hit the animal? I personally stick with fixed broadheads. Check out those QuickHits," he said, pointing. "They're new and are supposed to make a fast, ethical kill."

"Great, thank you. I'll get them!" Kay grabbed the package of QuickHits off the rack. "Hey, do you guys have bear spray?"

Kay had been internally grappling with the idea of going bowhunting tomorrow morning. Going hunting early was her original plan. It was Saturday, so she could sit in the tree all day if she wanted to, and it was the first week of November—prime rut time—perfect for whitetail hunting. But now she had this mangy… bear… lurking around. Kay concluded she would buy some bear spray and hunt on the other side of the property tomorrow.

"Oh yeah, over here."

Kay followed Nick to the back corner of the store.

"Did you see a bear?" he asked.

"Yeah… well… I don't know." She didn't know why she
answered like that. She always seemed to tell Nick more
than she wanted to.

"It looked like a bear, but it was so distant. I only saw it
through binoculars. The only thing was that it was
deformed or something. Like it had strange proportions and
these big black eyes. I only spotted it for a few seconds up
in a pine tree. It should have broken the branch but
seemed… weightless."

Oh my gosh, why was she telling him all of this? She
probably sounded insane.

Nick answered softly, "Hmmm, well, the Department of
Natural Resources has been reporting some weird animal
activity in Owlsbourne recently, wildlife not migrating
normally and avoiding their usual nesting and bedding
areas. Maybe it's a new disease or something? Just make
sure that you inspect whatever deer you shoot before
processing and eating it. And keep this bear spray on you at
all times. A few people have come in here mentioning
some lingering black bears that are gathering a bit more
food before hibernation."

Nick was always so understanding, and he never judged.
That's probably why Kay trusted him. Nick Knight was
effortlessly good-looking. His black Shadowflight
employee T-shirt was tucked into tight, straight-leg blue
jeans. He was a few inches taller than Kay; he had a sturdy,
strong build. Nick's dark brown hair was always a little
messy—in a good way, like he just ran a hand through it
and called it a day. His eyes were deep brown and serious,

like he was always thinking about something bigger than what was in front of him. His skin was a warm golden tone. The stubble on his face perfectly framed his square jawline. Nick was rough around the edges but solid. His crooked, mischievous grin revealed a warm smile. He was striking.

Kay liked Nick. She had always had a little crush on him.

He was an enigma to Kay. Nick was super intelligent, handsome, an incredible archer, and an all-around capable guy. But when they were in middle school together, Nick got in big trouble. He broke into and robbed a local convenience store. He started hanging out with the wrong crowd when they were about twelve years old, and by the time he robbed that store at fifteen, he had already committed too many crimes to count. The town gossip was that he was doing drugs then, too.

The only reason Nick wasn't shipped off to the juvenile detention center in Hartford was because his dad was the sheriff of Owlsbourne, and everyone loved him.

Marcus Knight was a legend in Owlsbourne. He was celebrity-handsome (no question where Nick got his good looks). He cleaned up homelessness and crime in Owlsbourne. Owlsbourne renamed the town green "Knight Park" in honor of his career. He died several years ago in a sudden and tragic car accident that had the town reeling for months.

So how did Marcus get a criminal son? Too much privilege was the town's consensus. Nonetheless, Nick got himself straight and graduated from Owlsbourne High at the top of their class. He had been working at Shadowflight ever since.

Kay followed Nick back to the cash register in front of the store. Nick rang up the QuickHits and bear spray.

"All right, it'll be $29.99."

"That's not right. The QuickHits alone are $35," Kay corrected.

Nick looked up from the register and smiled, his white teeth glimmering under the slant of his lips. "Did you think I forgot? I know it's your birthday, Kay. You've been coming here every year, on this day, for as long as I've been working here. The QuickHits are on me. Now go get that big one tomorrow." He winked. His fingers brushed her hand as he handed her the bag.

Just then, the BlackHole holiday advertisement came on the store radio.

"Hi folks! Siren Hex speaking. You know me as the Founder of BlackHole, but did you also know that Thanksgiving is my and my daughter's favorite holiday? What better way to show our appreciation for Owlsbourne and our love of this day than our annual BlackHole Turkey Giving! Be sure to pick up your free turkey at the Owlsbourne Bob's Corner Grocer before they're all gone! From all of us here at BlackHole, thank you! Remember, we're wiring minds for tomorrow!"

Kay made a gagging motion in front of Nick.

"What is that slogan about? Wiring minds? So creepy," Nick laughed.

"They're coming for your brain!" Kay taunted as she raised her hands and wiggled her fingers. "Ooooo."

"Thank you for everything. I'll text you when I get that big buck!" Kay shouted back to Nick and walked out the front door just as Alabama started singing "Dixieland Delight" over the store speakers.

That animal was just so… weird… this morning… Bear spray will take care of it, bear or not, she thought to herself as she climbed into the Jeep, placed her bags on the passenger seat, and buckled her seatbelt.

Kay hit the gas and floored it out of the Shadowflight Archery parking lot toward her parents' house.

Chapter 7

6:19 p.m. – "Oh, you're early…" her mom was surprised as Kay walked through the door. "Well, in that case, grab some plates and help me set the table. Your brother and sister will be here soon. The cleaner forgot to put all the plates out like I asked her to. I swear, it is impossible to find good help."

Kay said nothing as she took the plates from the cabinet and set the table.

"No! Not those plates! Honestly, Kay, have some standards. This is a family dinner. Get the nice plates out of the china cabinet."

That almost sounded like a "Happy Birthday, Kay!"

Kay slumped over to the china cabinet.

Kay's "standards" were never quite up to par in her mother's eyes. Pam McQuinn deplored Kay's tattoos, band tees, and combat boots. Pam couldn't stand bowhunting. Pam told Kay once that she was "not proud" of Kay for bowhunting.

Pam loved her daughter, but with conditions. Kay and Pam's relationship was akin to Lorelai and Emily Gilmore's.

Pam expected Kay to be married now with kids. Simply put, she pictured Kay as someone else. And throughout Kay's life, Pam reluctantly accepted the parts of Kay she thought were less than ideal.

Amid an argument once, Kay said to her mom, "I know I am not the daughter that you imagined."

To which Pam immediately responded, "No, no, you are not. You couldn't be further from the daughter that I dreamed of."

Kay folded the birthday-themed napkins and placed them in each spot on the table.

Pam's dyed blonde, newly trimmed, blow-dried hair swished on her shoulders as she pulled the meal out of the oven. Her floral-printed eyeglasses hung around her neck, clacking against some chunky, expensive jewelry. Her glasses normally framed her watchful, wide eyes that never missed anything—especially not your mistakes. She wore a gauzy, paisley blouse; her lipstick was always just a touch too bold, and her expression carried the weight of a thousand unspoken judgments.

"What's up, kiddo?" Bruce McQuinn approached from the stairwell.

"Hi, Dad! Not much," Kay answered.

"Happy Birthday! We love you! Thirty is a big one!" Bruce exclaimed as he embraced his daughter in a giant bear hug, her face squished against his brawny chest.

Bruce was six foot three inches; his broad shoulders and strong build commanded the attention of every room, and his raven-black hair was now peppered with streaks of silver. It was thick and carefully styled—slicked back. He had a distinct, hook-shaped, two-inch scar on the back of his right hand—a souvenir from the slip of a skinning knife while processing a deer when he was younger.

Bruce had a warm smile and a jolly laugh. But now he was a shadow of the man he used to be. The years had caught up with him. Heavy creases carved deep lines into his forehead and around his eyes—eyes that had once been sharp and commanding, now sat dulled and ringed with shadows that no amount of sleep could erase. He wore an oversized button-up shirt to hide the weight he had gained. His skin was pale. Bruce didn't look great. Kay figured that was because he was drinking again.

Aside from Dee, Bruce taught Kay a lot of what she knew. He, too, was an excellent bowhunter. He climbed up the corporate ladder as a lab rat. Bruce had a degree in chemical engineering. He built his entire career on nothing but hard work and grit. Kay admired her father so much. She had fond memories of her dad, from building treehouses to painting a *Lion King* mural in Kay's childhood bedroom.

"That's enough, you two! Luke and Zoey are going to be here any second! Fill the water glasses, please!"

Bruce winked at Kay as she picked up the glass water pitcher and started pouring.

Every gathering in the McQuinn household was an event. According to Pam, there was no such thing as a casual hangout. While this was not Kay's style, the effort made for some great memories growing up. Every holiday was a spectacle. Pam always decorated the house beautifully and made sure it was a memorable day.

At dinner, Luke, Kay's younger brother, rambled on about his recent travels abroad.

"And then we stayed in a beautiful hotel overlooking the Amalfi Coast," he explained while he shoveled forkfuls of penne into his mouth. Kay watched the food get pulverized by his molars as he kept talking.

"It was really something. Kay, why don't you plan a trip there? It's honestly so beautiful. Traveling would do you some good. Get out of this small town for a while, clear your head," he continued, through a mouthful of pasta. His lanky elbows rested on the table, and his long, black hair swung in front of his eyes. He had his striped linen shirt unbuttoned at the chest, with a shell necklace that he picked up in Hawaii dangling above the plate of pasta. He smelled faintly of weed. Luke was the kind of brother who disappeared for months, then showed up unannounced with a story about a desert commune, a failed band, or a girl he barely remembered.

Luke and Kay were buddies. They talked a lot on the phone, and she heard all about his travels. He didn't have his own place; Luke just stayed with his parents when he was in town, which wasn't often. He fancied himself a nomad. "What else are your twenties for?" Luke had declared more than once.

Kay respected traveling, but his nomadic lifestyle was only possible because Bruce footed most of Luke's bills.

"Yeah, I'd like to go. Maybe one day," Kay answered. She wasn't hungry. All she could think about was her morning hunt and that bear.

In Luke's world, people could do whatever they wanted, whenever they wanted. Money was not an issue. *What a world,* Kay thought.

"I'm so happy that my trip timing worked out, and I'll be in town for the Bicentennial! I'll get to see everyone in town! I can't wait to tell them all about my travels. I want to encourage these people to leave town and get out more!" Luke said to no one. He was so disconnected from reality. As if the townspeople needed his insight to travel—like that was the missing puzzle piece, not them actually needing money and time off from work.

"I didn't make garlic bread because I figured we all didn't need it," Pam interjected.

No one had asked where the garlic bread was. It was no secret that Pam thought Kay should be thinner. She wanted Kay to be skinny, "like when Kay lived in Philadelphia." Pam had stated this several times. "Why don't you try eating like you did when you were making your art? You looked so good! I just want you to be healthy. Are you at your heaviest weight now?" That was a conversation from a few weeks ago. Little did Pam know, Kay was also suicidal when she was at her skinniest because the nerves made eating impossible. But looks very much mattered to Pam—looks and status.

"I think everything tastes great! Thank you, honey," Bruce jumped in, trying to soften the blow of his wife's never-ending critiques. He poured himself yet another glass of Cabernet Sauvignon. Kay noticed the tremor in Bruce's hand as he lifted the bottle. She also caught Pam glaring at him from across the table. *That'll be a fight after we leave,* Kay thought. Last time Kay was here, she had found Bruce's five-year sobriety chip forgotten in a kitchen drawer, somewhere between the staples and rubber bands.

Not reading the room, Luke jumped in, "Actually, Mom, this is really delicious. But I had some of the best pasta in Italy. Like you wouldn't believe how good it was!" He continued chewing with his mouth open, unaware of the flicker of hurt that passed through Pam's eyes.

Zoey noticed. "Still, nothing is better than homemade! Thank you again for cooking, Mom."

Zoey was the apple of Pam's eye. Zoey never grew out of that first-child role. She was a people pleaser and her parents' most accomplished kid, by McQuinn standards. Zoey was a partner at a local law firm and pregnant with her third child. She was athletic, successful, and a bit of a know-it-all. Being a know-it-all was warranted, as she was also valedictorian of her high school class and graduated from Yale Law School with straight A's.

Zoey and Kay had a special bond. For one thing, they both remembered what it was like to be poor before their dad's success. They would reminisce about the fancy hot dog dinners Pam fixed for them when they were all living in a broken-down trailer in East Owlsbourne. These were memories Luke couldn't relate to.

Zoey and Kay also shared music recommendations and talked about movies. Zoey greatly appreciated all things pop culture. They loved each other very much but were very different people: Kay, the wayward, haphazard artist, and Zoey, the straight-laced, by-the-book achiever.

"Thank you, Mom. You know, this meat sauce is my favorite. It's been a really great birthday," Kay said graciously.

She meant it. Her mom's cooking was unparalleled. Kay was thankful to have a family that cared about her so much that, despite their imperfections, they threw her a birthday party with ice cream cake at thirty years old.

Pam was a lot of things, but most of all, she was a loving mother who, despite her hurtful comments, filled the house with warmth. Pam was also an incredibly talented artist, but came from a generation that did not encourage women to pursue their passions. Her years of painting watercolor landscapes were far behind her.

Kay picked up her plate and cleared the rest of the dishes from the table to prepare for dessert.

"Kay, don't do that. It's your birthday," Bruce demanded.

"That's okay, you know me—I actually like cleaning," Kay answered. She really did.

Kay stuck her spoon into the blue, gooey "A" on her piece of Carvel ice cream cake as she opened her gifts. Her presents consisted of a "very expensive," high-end sweater that Kay would never wear from Pam and Bruce, an original, perfect-condition vinyl of *Cat Stevens' Tea for the Tillerman* from Zoey, and an "I owe you" from Luke.

"Thank you, guys! I love you all."

After helping clean up, Kay stepped outside to see her dad smoking a vape on the patio. She sat next to him on one of the wrought-iron benches Pam had lining their rose garden.

"How are you doing, kiddo?" He blew a cloud of tobacco-scented vapor into the air. The red wine stained his lips. He was a little tipsy. Kay knew this because Bruce was not chatty; he had a lot on his mind with work, but he always became friendlier as he drank.

"I'm doing okay," Kay answered. "I'm optimistic that I'll get that big buck in the morning. You know, the one I text you trailcam photos of."

Bruce was the only family member who supported whatever Kay wanted to accomplish. He especially supported bowhunting because he was a hunter himself before work stole all his time. Dee was his mom and his hunting partner back in the day.

Bruce's father, Stan McQuinn, had heart disease and eventually died from a heart attack many years earlier. Losing Stan devastated Kay's family and—most importantly and most heartbreakingly—Dee.

Stan was tough. He was a veteran of the Second World War and had weathered many storms in his life. He rarely ever expressed emotion. Kay didn't even remember him talking very much at all. His face constantly expressed a quiet scrutiny, continuously measuring the world against an invisible standard few could meet. The only time Stan ever smiled was when he saw Dee.

Bruce had always chased Stan's approval—that much was clear. In that way, he and Kay weren't so different. Both carried a quiet ache for affirmation. Just as Bruce longed for his father to be proud of him, Kay only ever wanted Bruce to be proud of her.

"That deer is a beast! You're going to get him. I know you are. I can't wait to grill up the backstraps with you. You're doing great. You're amazing, kiddo." His eyes had a slight alcohol-induced haze, but Kay knew that he really meant it. With Bruce, alcohol was a truth serum. He said the most genuine and helpful things when buzzed. Kay just sometimes wished that he would say them when he was sober.

"Fred tells me you've been making beautiful designs lately." Yes, that Fred. "You know you're always welcome to come work for my team. The role might not be exactly what you imagined, but it would pay more, and you'd have some more creative control."

All Kay wanted to do was leave Owlsbourne behind and remove herself from this filthy corporate circle, but here she was, right back in it. She was once a rolling stone, exploring and in love with life. Now she felt like a heavy boulder, covered in moss and bugs, worn from time and… stuck. She was a forgotten place where people would stop to tie their shoelaces on their way up the mountain.

"Thanks, Dad. I'll keep that in mind."

"Why don't you make more of your incredible art, Kay?" Bruce asked. "You can't let some internet trolls and BlackHole stop you forever. You've got to keep moving forward."

Bruce was resilient, just like Dee.

When BlackHole stole her ideas, he helped pay for an attorney to fight BlackHole. It was still a futile battle, but she appreciated his support. He had even done research within BlackHole, but only got so far before being warned not to get involved.

"I don't know, Dad. I feel worthless now. Like the interest in my art was a fad or something," Kay answered honestly.

Bruce put his giant arm around Kay and pulled her close. "No, no, enough with the pity party. You are special, and so is your art. Other people see that. It's time for you to see it too, Kay. I know that you're going to be something great. Keep working hard. You'll get there."

"I Venmoed you $500 during dinner," he let go and looked her in the eyes.

"What?! Dad, please don't do that. You did not need to do that," Kay replied, nearly yelling.

"I know, I know. But look, you never ask me for anything. Let me give you this little birthday present. Plus, I know you're never going to wear that sweater that Mom got you."

He was right about that.

"Wow, Dad. Okay… thank you. That is so generous. I love you." She squeezed him tight and felt relief wash over her, thinking about the bills she could cover with that money. The phone company had been threatening to shut off her cell service since Monday.

Chapter 8

9:19 p.m. – On the way home, Kay stopped at the
Owlsbourne Cemetery. She did this every year on her
birthday. A few years prior, her best friend, Penny, passed
away from a drug overdose.

Penny Grant was a jock. She was extroverted, had a great
sense of humor, and always volunteered for school
activities, unlike Kay. Kay had hung around with the artist
types. Despite their differences, Penny and Kay became
fast friends in Ms. Palmer's sixth-grade homeroom when
they discovered they shared a birthday. Through high
school and college, they remained close friends.

Penny was the person who made living seem fun and easy.
She lit up every room she walked into. She made light of
any situation, no matter how dire it felt. Penny was always
smiling and laughing. Penny had never even thought about
getting a tattoo. She was clean-cut and beautiful. She had
long, black, glossy hair—probably from her Japanese
heritage—soft features, and an athletic build. Her family
was put together and kind, too. They were the kind of
family you read about in books or saw in movies, the
American Dream—but they were real.

"Hey, buddy," Kay said as she approached the fresh
headstone. She gently dusted some dirt off the top of it.
"Happy Birthday."

"I miss you." Kay clutched the silver wolf necklace around her neck. The necklace had been a gift from Penny's mom after Penny's passing. Wolves were Penny's favorite animal. Etched into the back of the wolf silhouette were the initials K+P, Kay and Penny.

Penny didn't do drugs, but in college, she and Kay experimented a bit. It was a bad batch of ecstasy that ended Penny's life. Just a stupid mistake. One dumb decision. Penny didn't have a drug habit; that was the first time she had ever tried ecstasy.

"I'm getting there. I got a job as a 'designer.' It's not exactly what I dreamed of or what we always talked about, but it's paying the bills—kind of," Kay updated Penny's headstone. "And Nick Knight gave me a birthday gift," Kay grinned, as her cheeks flushed. "I know you would have been jealous of that," she teased.

Penny loved Kay's art and always encouraged Kay to pursue an art career. "You're a brilliant artist! Come on, nothing ventured, nothing gained." Penny helped Kay create her art PicsPost account and was there when Kay posted her first original piece online. Man, Penny would have gone nuts over the attention Kay's art eventually got, and she would have somehow made the BlackHole experience seem like a funny story to tell after a few drinks.

"I love you," Kay said, laying her hand on the cold, wet granite. Then, she pulled out her phone and texted Penny's parents, like she did every year.

"Love you guys. I hope you had a nice day. Thinking of you. <3 Kay"

Kay saw the time on her screen; she had to get home to walk Shotgun. Carlo took him out this afternoon so Kay could go to dinner, but now she was pushing it with time.

On her way out of the cemetery, Kay spotted a tall, angular figure moving between the graves. He carried a shovel, dragging it behind him, the metal scraping softly against a gravel path. He wore what looked like a dirty groundskeeper's uniform.

He didn't see her.

Or maybe he did and didn't care.

Then he muttered words she couldn't hear and started digging. Jonny Langley, the town loner, worked a lot of odd jobs. Apparently, the gravedigger at the Owlsbourne Cemetery was his newest gig.

Kay quietly shut the rusted gate and walked toward her car in the parking lot.

Kay's apartment was in East Owlsbourne, a rough part of town.

9:50 p.m. – Flickering streetlights cast uneven pools of light on the abandoned storefronts and graffiti-covered walls. Paint peeled off the weathered buildings, and cracked sidewalks accompanied the narrow streets, showing the scars of years of neglect. Food trucks and smokers lined her block. This was where you could find the best tacos in Connecticut. Kay parked her car under an Allerzil billboard on Ivy Street and walked over to the Sombrero Supremo truck.

"What's up, Juan? I'll take my usual."

"Hi, Kay! You got it! Two carne asada tacos coming up!"

Juan walked to the back of the truck to cook.

Sombrero Supremo and Chappell Roan's *The Rise and Fall of a Midwest Princess* were the only two things that kept Kay going these days.

The bear from earlier that morning was out of Kay's mind now. Instead, her mind swirled with memories of Penny, doubts about her life, and the hope that maybe she'd be able to create beautiful art again one day.

"Here you go! I threw in some guac and chips, on the house," Juan winked at her as he handed her the greasy, red-checkered paper food tray.

"You're the best," Kay thanked him as she left a 50% tip on her credit card receipt.

As soon as Kay entered her second-floor apartment, she was mauled by an insanely happy Shotgun. She loved him so much.

"Okay, okay! Here's a treat, bud! Let's go potty."

She clipped the leash on his collar as she gave him a dog biscuit, and took him down the two flights of outdoor stairs toward the small patch of grass behind their apartment complex.

"Hey, Maya! What are you up to?"

Kay looked down at the eight-year-old girl sitting on the bottom stair of the stairwell, playing *Tetris* on an original Game Boy. The girl's black hair hung in her face. Her too-short sweatpants exposed her sockless ankles. The rubber soles of her once-white tennis shoes were visibly peeling off. When she looked up at Kay, her face was distant and covered in a thin layer of dirt, like it hadn't been washed in weeks.

"Hi, Kay! I think tonight I'm finally going to break my high score!" Maya replied excitedly.

"I bet you will! That's amazing! Do you want a blanket and a cereal bar? Your favorite, Fruity O's flavor!"

This had become Kay's ritual, giving Maya a blanket and some food at night. Kay didn't know why Maya didn't want to go into her apartment. She had never seen Maya's parents. Kay had anonymously called Child Protective Services several times for a welfare check on Maya, but nothing had ever come of it.

"Wow, if you don't mind, that would be awesome. Thank you, Kay, you're the best!" Maya answered gratefully.

"Here, hold Shotgun's leash for a second." Kay ran back up the stairs into her apartment to grab a small knit blanket and two cereal bars, then headed back down the stairs.

When she returned, Maya was hugging Shotgun. "You are the cutest boy."

"Here you go! Go ahead and keep the blanket," Kay said.

Kay said this every night, and every morning she would find the blanket perfectly folded and gently placed outside her front door.

"Good luck with your high score." Kay grabbed Shotgun's leash and took him to the grass to do his business.

Once back inside, Kay switched off the thrift store lamp, which was just a dusty bulb without a shade. Then, she and Shotgun curled up on her Craigslist queen mattress on the floor. She pulled the teal fleece blanket over both of them, placed the tacos on her lap (ready to eat), and turned on *Alien* on her laptop.

For a moment, Kay reflected on her position in life. She was poor, in debt from legal fees and student loans, thirty years old, single, and renting a room in the absolute worst part of town. She couldn't get her art career off the ground. Maybe she should take that job offer from Bruce to work at BlackHole. She mentally berated herself until her eyes fluttered shut.

Kay and Shotgun were snoring before Sigourney ever discovered the Xenomorph.

Chapter 9

SATURDAY

4:00 a.m. – Kay slapped her alarm clock and groggily dragged Shotgun outside.

"Come on, Shotgun. We've got to get moving. Today is the day that I get that big buck!"

She was so excited. Nothing made her happier than spending time in the woods.

Kay brewed up some instant coffee, ate a s'mores Pop-Tart and an apple (an unusually healthy addition to her candy-addicted diet), took a quick shower with scent killer body wash, suited up in all her heavyweight camo gear, and hung her lucky wolf around her neck.

"Wish me luck, big guy. Love you!" she whispered to Shotgun as she gently closed the door, careful not to wake her roommate, Carlo.

5:05 a.m. – It was dark, very dark. Kay grabbed her compound bow from the backseat and gingerly closed the car door. Silence was so crucial while hunting. All her senses were turned on.

She parked in front of Dee's old cabin again. The clearing in the woods allowed the moonlight to wash over the entire property. Kay looked up at the stars in the sky before trudging into the black forest.

"Good morning, Big Dipper," she whispered.

Today, she planned on sitting on the opposite side of the property. She wanted to minimize the risk of running into that bear.

Kay snapped her bino pack onto her chest, placed the bear spray in her largest pocket, adjusted her bibs, turned on her green flashlight, and started walking down the trail— opposite yesterday's trail.

The air was cool and crisp, as leaves crunched under the weight of her 2,000-gram hunting boots. The woods were always mysterious, but in the dark, at this hour, the mystery became almost threatening. Kay couldn't see six feet in front of her. It's amazing what the human mind will invent when it cannot see its surroundings. That's the thing about the dark—in the dark, even the most beautiful tree can look like a bloodthirsty, grimacing monster.

A few beams of moonlight broke through the canopy, casting a slight glow on the underbrush. Kay felt at peace, like she was a part of whatever secrets the forest held.

Finally, after slowly, quietly walking for about ten minutes, she spotted the sheen of metal from her ladder stand.

Kay clumsily climbed up the rungs with all her equipment and settled on the frigid, hard metal seat. She touched the bear spray in her pocket for reassurance. Then, she leaned back against the tree trunk and let out a long exhale. This was her favorite—being out here, in these trees.

For the next few hours, Kay could watch the world come alive, all alone, with no stressful interruptions—just her and nature.

Kay tilted her head back against the tree and started spotting constellations. She loved looking up. Occasionally, she would catch a shooting star, and in more recent years, she would spot satellites and sometimes the International Space Station.

She heard a loud scurry. She peered below her stand to see a raccoon looking right at her. Its beady eyes glowed in the moonlight. She quickly turned on her green flashlight to spook the raccoon. It worked, and he ran off.

"Forget the bear—the last thing I need is a raccoon climbing this ladder and attacking me," Kay said aloud to no one.

5:45 a.m. – Kay had nodded off for just a moment. The quiet chirp of the crickets and the still, frigid air put her to sleep. Thank goodness she was harnessed to the tree with a safety system.

When Kay snapped awake, she saw the silhouette of a barred owl perched on a bare branch across from her— another beautiful moment for her memory bank.

The owl's head seemed to move slightly, maybe looking for prey. An unlucky mouse? Then its head hinged backward, looking toward the stars. Kay followed its gaze.

Above them, another satellite was streaking across the sky. Kay watched as the shining orb slowly moved from right to left on its preprogrammed mission.

Kay noticed the crickets had stopped chirping. The woods were completely silent, like someone had hit the mute button. Then, the owl spread its wings and flew off.

How gorgeous, Kay thought.

She looked back up at the sky. The satellite was still floating by, but it seemed to move a little slower than most satellites—and it had gotten bigger.

"Huh," Kay said out loud.

Right when Kay said that, the satellite stopped above her treestand.

Kay grabbed her phone, thinking she could use her Sky Map app to figure out what was flying above her.

Before she could open the app, her phone was drenched in a radiant, white glow. She looked back up toward the satellite, but all she saw was a blinding light. Her entire body suddenly felt weightless.

Then her world went black.

Chapter 10

"What the…?" Kay muttered as she opened her eyes. The sun was glaring above her. She squinted. The sunlight danced on the frost covering the frozen ground beneath her back. Her bow and phone lay beside her, just out of reach of her left hand.

Kay rolled onto her side. "Ow!" she yelled as she grabbed her left shoulder; it was tender and sore. Did she fall from her treestand? What happened?

She slowly sat up. *Okay, don't panic.*

She stood up and brushed the dirt off her jacket and pants. Birds chirped overhead.

What time is it? She looked down at her watch, 8:22 a.m.

"That's impossible." She vaguely recalled a white light, weightlessness, then nothing. "I must have fallen asleep and fallen out of my treestand. Maybe my hunter safety strap snapped."

She looked at the strap attached to her back, and it was intact.

She picked up her phone off the ground, stood up, and carefully climbed up to the top of the treestand ladder to inspect the safety anchor strap that was wrapped around the tree. The anchor strap was also intact, but the metal carabiner that she clipped her strap into was melted. Kay looked closer. The metal was still glowing orange with heat. It looked like it was forged into the bark of the tree.

She used her phone to take several photos of the scene so she could analyze them later. Right now, she figured it would be wise to get out of the treestand in case the stand had some kind of issue and was the reason she fell.

Kay glanced at the rest of the ladder on her way down. Nothing else seemed to be out of place. She touched the bear spray in her pocket for some peace of mind.

"Okay… what happened?" she recounted aloud. "I nodded off for a second, then I woke up and saw the owl. That was probably around 6:00 a.m. I didn't fall asleep for more than fifteen minutes, if even. I watched the owl, then spotted another satellite. Man, it was all so quick. The satellite stopped. That was weird. I grabbed my phone to map which satellite it was, and when I looked back up—flash. That's all I remember. Could it all have been a dream? It certainly didn't feel like a dream."

Suddenly, the world was spinning, and she felt like she was going to throw up.

Kay collected her things. Her hunt was busted now. Her shoulder was throbbing. Confused, frustrated, and a little freaked out, she made the trek back to her car, her mind racing as she walked. All she could remember was that owl and the bright light.

"Kay, get a grip on yourself. Missing time? Bright lights? You sound like a lunatic from some backwoods YouTube video. You must have dozed off. But why the melted carabiner? Maybe it was like that, and you didn't notice it in the dark? That doesn't make sense. I remember clipping myself into it."

She gave herself a pep talk all the way back to the car, clutching her compound bow, which seemed to be undamaged, in her left hand and the bear spray in her right.

"Fuck."

8:58 a.m. – She turned the key, and the car came to life. Kay wanted to panic. She started sweating, her stomach turned, the whole world started spinning again, and wild, intrusive thoughts flooded her mind. She squeezed her eyes closed in desperation.

Breathe... it'll pass.

Her eyes welled with tears. Once her heart rate slowed, she opened her eyes.

"You must have fallen asleep. That's it."

With that, the Jeep Cherokee rolled away from Dee's cabin once again, with no buck in the truck.

Chapter 11

Kay turned up the static radio.

"Hi folks! Siren Hex speaking. You all know me as the President of BlackHole, but did y—"

"Shut up!" Kay shouted as she smacked the power button. Her brain felt as windy as the back roads she was carving the Jeep through.

She passed the well-known Owlsbourne speed trap, which would normally be an insignificant detail, but today it was very significant.

The next few moments changed Kay's life forever.

Kay glanced over at the state trooper, who was half-asleep in the front seat of his Crown Vic.

She looked back at the road through the windshield. She just had to get home to Shotgun. Kay was still confused about what happened this morning, but at least she hadn't come across that mangy bear.

About a mile past the speed trap, Kay stopped at the red light that led into the center of Owlsbourne. She glanced to her right and noticed a beat-up black SUV creaking to a halt next to her. The driver appeared to be flustered, and beside him, through the SUV window, she spotted a gray duffle bag ominously slouched on the passenger seat.

Then Kay blinked… just a normal, everyday blink. But today, after falling from that tree in the woods, the blink was different.

Blinking, with her eyes shut, Kay suddenly saw, in her mind, two clammy hands that she did not recognize gripping a steering wheel.

With her eyes still shut, Kay smelled stale cigarette smoke and mildew. She noticed discarded fast-food wrappers littering the floor of a vehicle that wasn't hers. She heard heavy breathing and distant heavy metal music. Then, on her right, she noticed the weathered, canvas-gray duffle bag in the passenger seat. Suddenly, she heard, "Fuck it! I'm going to run this light—that cop knows!" from a grumbly, scared male voice.

Kay opened her eyes. She was still sitting in her Cherokee at the red light. What did she just see, or imagine? Then, out of nowhere, the SUV's wheels next to her car screeched as the SUV unexpectedly sped through the red light.

"Hold on… what?" Kay whispered, and overwhelming, mind-numbing uncertainty gripped her. "What the hell is happening?! Did I see inside that guy's car? Like, actually see from the inside of his car?"

Kay was a very visual thinker. Many of her most creative ideas came to her like watching a television in her mind. That is exactly how she described it to her mom when she was younger. She could always envision her art in her mind before ever putting it down on paper or on a screen. That, she figured, was probably what made her such a good designer.

She was also very familiar with intrusive visual thoughts because of her obsessive-compulsive disorder.

What just happened was sort of like that… but very different. This time, Kay could see, hear, and smell a whole scene that seemed to be actually happening in the physical world. On top of that, she felt the emotions that she was imagining. Stress.

Her art ideas and unwanted OCD thoughts were never like *that*.

This experience was new and unlike anything she had ever experienced before.

Kay was disoriented. She felt trapped in her uncertainty, locked in her car, and suddenly claustrophobic.

"Don't panic."

By now, she was ready to have a full-on heart attack.

Between the lost time, bright white light, melted metal, and this, Kay was ready to drive straight to the hospital and commit herself.

A few moments later, she heard a siren. Then she blinked.

This time, when Kay blinked, she instantly saw two abnormally large, hairy, male hands gripping a steering wheel. She smelled a sweetness in the air. Maybe donuts? In front of her, she witnessed a road quickly disappearing under the hood of a white police vehicle. To the left, on the road ahead, was the back of a green Jeep Cherokee. One of the abnormally large hands reached down and grabbed a walkie.

Kay heard, "I'm in pursuit! Send back up! I think this is our guy!"

Through the vision, Kay felt a body that was sweaty and pumped up on adrenaline.

Then, she opened her eyes. She was still in her Jeep Cherokee, now sitting at a green light, as a cop car whizzed by on her right in pursuit of the SUV.

"Holy shit," Kay whispered. Something was wrong.

A car she hadn't noticed was sitting a few feet behind her.

The driver honked, and Kay pressed the gas.

Chapter 12

The short ride home from Dee's cabin was a blur. It seemed like every time Kay blinked, she saw some foreign scene in her mind, all equally realistic and intrusive. Each scene seemed to correlate directly with people Kay could visibly see in the physical world, when her eyes were open. Driving through the center of Owlsbourne was the absolute worst. Every time she blinked, she saw something new in her mind.

Something else that Kay noted was that even though the visions felt long and detailed, when she opened her eyes, she didn't seem to lose time. She had her eyes closed for as long as a normal blink. So, the visions had to be slightly in the future or in the past.

Kay was shaken and desperate to get to her apartment to grab Shotgun and some clothes, then head back to the woods. It seemed like whatever was going on with her was being sparked by her proximity to people.

Kay found a parking spot. She was trying desperately to keep her eyes wide open. Kay was playing a game of don't blink with herself. Sweat poured down her forehead. She was in full-on fight-or-flight mode. Tears trickled down her cheeks, but she did not blink. She squeezed her wolf necklace for comfort.

"Hi Kay! We have a new special today! Want to try it? On the house, of course," Juan offered as she speed-walked by the food truck.

"Uh, maybe next time! Thanks, Juan!" Kay shouted dismissively as she nearly ran by. Her only focus was getting into her apartment.

Kay blinked. No intrusive visions this time. She noted this discrepancy and rushed toward the outdoor stairwell.

As Kay approached the apartment building, she blinked again, and, this time, she saw, in her mind, small, dirty hands pounding on a slatted door.

"Mom, please, please let me out! I promise that I'll behave!"

Dim light filtered through the slats, and Kay saw musty, beaten boxes stacked on the sides of what seemed to be the inside of a dark closet. She smelled wet, moldy carpet. The air was stale. Then, she spotted, from inside the closet, the chain of a bike lock securing the closet doors together. On a stack of battered shoeboxes, Kay noticed an original Game Boy.

"Maya!" Kay opened her eyes and shouted out loud. Instinctively, she sprinted to apartment eighty-seven, where Maya lived. Kay knocked. No answer. She heard rustling on the other side of the door.

Kay blinked. Suddenly, she felt warm tears roll down her cheeks—or the cheeks of the person in her vision—and

Kay felt an overwhelming sadness. The small hands in her vision wiped away tears as the person leaned forward to peer through the slats.

Kay opened her eyes again. She couldn't control what she was seeing or feeling; Kay seemed to only be a passenger to the visions.

Kay called 911 this time. If Maya was in trouble, Kay needed to help her. All of Kay's previous anonymous calls to Child Protective Services had gone nowhere. Kay gave the dispatcher the location and details of the abuse she thought was happening.

"I am going to look unhinged if nothing is happening in this apartment," Kay thought.

Five long minutes later, the police rolled up. Kay paced, waiting in the stairwell while the cops entered apartment eighty-seven. Shotgun could wait just a few more minutes.

Kay heard a woman screaming, and she heard fighting from inside the apartment.

Then the cops marched out with a disheveled, forty-something-year-old lady in handcuffs.

"I know my rights!" the woman snarled at one of the police officers.

Exiting the apartment, behind the woman, was Maya, in tattered dinosaur-print pajamas, holding the Game Boy, walking next to a crisis intervention officer.

"Maya!" Kay instinctively ran over to the girl and hugged her tightly. "Are you okay?"

"Hi Kay. I'm okay." Maya squeezed back. "My mom needs some help, and these people say they're going to help her. I am going to stay with my aunt in Derry, Maine, for a bit." Maya looked toward the crisis officer for reassurance.

"That's right, we've already spoken to her aunt, and everything is all set up. It should be a fun adventure!" The officer looked toward Maya warmly. "How about you go get a candy bar from Officer Jones over there while I talk to Ms. Kay?"

"Okay," Maya agreed and wandered toward the back of the patrol car.

"Hi, Ms. McQuinn. It's my understanding that you placed the call to 911?"

"Yes," Kay responded. Her mind was racing. Was she seeing other people's real-time perspectives? How was she sure that Maya was in trouble? Was this all a dream?

"Thank goodness you called us," the officer said graciously. "It looks like that young girl has been neglected and locked in a closet countless times as punishment."

A closet! Holy shit! Kay screamed in her mind. That's exactly what she saw in her vision.

"Her mother has a lot of explaining to do and will not be allowed near Maya for the foreseeable future."

"Wow. I thought I heard chaos inside. I wanted to get help here, just in case. Thank you all for showing up. Please let me know if you need anything else from me." With that, Kay handed the officer her cell phone number and pretended to casually walk up the stairs to her apartment.

Everything in her body told her to run up the stairwell to Shotgun. This was all too much. But Kay kept her cool.

Kay reached her apartment door after what felt like an eternity. Again and again and again, when she blinked, she saw experiences that were not her own.

Chapter 13

"We're going on a trip, bud," Kay announced to Shotgun as she threw some clothes, toiletries, and more Pop-Tarts into a backpack.

She tried to stay quiet. Carlo had late shifts at the restaurant on weekends and was still sleeping. She sent him a text.

"Heading out for a few days. Wanted to let you know. Taking Shotgun with me. Have a great weekend!"

Her left shoulder was pulsing with pain. She must have hurt it when she fell out of the tree. She'd check it out when she got back to Dee's cabin.

Kay knelt down to clip on Shotgun's collar and quietly confided in him, "I think I might have finally gone crazy." He wagged his tail with delight. "I'm happy one of us finds it amusing," she told him as they exited the apartment.

9:58 a.m. – The gravel driveway crunched as the Jeep Cherokee squeaked to a halt. Kay knew that coming to Dee's cabin might not be the right move, since the mysterious occurrences were happening on that property, but it was where she felt safe. Plus, Dee's was far enough from people that she wasn't having any intrusive visions while blinking. That was Kay's theory at least, and, so far, it seemed to be true.

The cabin was nestled in the center of the sixty-acre plot. It was surrounded by tall, ancient trees that had endured the test of time. Their autumn-colored leaves were mostly gone by now. Barren, they stood like the protectors of Dee's home.

Kay inhaled the musk of pine, moss, and decaying leaves as she and Shotgun approached the neglected home. No one had tended to the cabin since Dee had died. Shingles were missing, and vines strangled the chimney. The log exterior was no longer a vibrant, natural chestnut hue. Instead, it had become a graying taupe. From the outside, the two-bedroom cabin looked like a scene from a horror movie.

But to Kay, it radiated love and good memories.

She knew the realtor's lockbox code and swung the front door open.

"Gross," Kay muttered immediately. The realtor had staged the craftsman cabin with modern, sterile decor that did not fit its rustic charm at all. On the hunter-green wallpapered accent wall, there were faint lines of dust where family photos used to hang. Covering some of the lines were newly hung, black-line paintings of flowers. Fortunately, the other walls were exposed knotty pine that the realtor couldn't ruin.

The one piece of Dee's art that the realtor kept on the wall was a large, engraved wood sign that read, "One Red Arrow Can Feed A Whole Village" in red block letters. Bruce had made this sign as a gift for his mother, Dee, in high school woodshop, and it had been hanging in Dee's cabin ever since—a constant reminder of her grandmother's favorite saying.

Kay walked inside and gently touched the doorframe of the small kitchen. The realtor had painted over the jagged pencil scratches that marked each new height milestone for Kay and her siblings.

She looked around at all the modern, stale furniture. The kitchen table had a glass top and gold-accented metal chairs. The staging furniture in the cabin was soulless.

Kay tossed her backpack onto the minimalist, neutral couch. She often wondered why people even bought modern furniture like that. It was never inviting to sit on. The new couch was the kind of furniture that, at one glance, you thought, "Wow, that looks insanely uncomfortable."

Shotgun liked the couch, though, and he quickly found himself a spot to roll around and chew the bone Kay packed for him.

"Good boy," Kay patted his head.

Then, Kay built a small fortress of logs in the wood-burning stove in the living room. She stuffed the log fortress with some kindling, tossed in a lit match, and latched the stove shut.

All of Dee's belongings had been boxed up and shoved into a dark, forgotten corner of the unfinished basement. It's amazing how an entire life can be broken down to a few dusty cardboard boxes that your kids bicker over and ultimately ignore.

She knew that no real estate showings were scheduled for the cabin until sometime during the week. Kay had been tracking the sale of this cabin for weeks because she did not want it to sell. Fortunately for her, most twenty-first-century couples did not want to hunt or farm and had no use (or budget) for sixty acres.

Sunlight poured in through the front windows, casting a warm glow on the rough wood floors. Dust particles twirled through the rays of light. Kay pulled out her laptop and set up camp on the mauve area rug in front of the couch.

"Okay, I am not 'seeing' anything in my mind now, while I'm here in the woods," she said aloud. "So, what is going on? Am I crazy?" She was fighting off waves of panic. Every few minutes, Kay would tremble as her chest tightened. Her thoughts were racing chaos, sweat beaded on her forehead, time warped, the room spun around her, and doom banged on the door in her brain. She squeezed her eyes shut briefly, fighting off a total existential meltdown.

Finally, she opened her laptop. It dinged immediately with new emails.

Most of the subject lines read something like, "Your Credit Card Payment is Now Past Due."

"Ugh," Kay ignored the demanding emails. She had maxed out all of her credit cards moving back to Owlsbourne a few years ago. Kay tuned out the screaming financial stress in her bones. She needed to focus on what was happening to her right now.

Time to distract her mind with an internet deep-dive.

Kay started by searching for any correlations between premonitions and lights in the sky. Unsurprisingly, she was bombarded with countless new-age, culty websites and message boards. The product recommendations on the web page advertisements were all for drug paraphernalia.

"Right… I have lost it," Kay accepted. She chewed on a strawberry Pop-Tart that she had packed. Kay wasn't even close to hungry, but she knew she had to eat.

She continued searching and combining different buzzwords and phrases: "satellites," "lost time," "melted metal," "white light," and more.

Then she searched "melted metal" and "Owlsbourne." Four search pages back, Kay stumbled upon a scan of an old news article from December 1989. Pictured in the article were the Bennett Boys smiling and holding up a large, cast bird foot—or that's what it appeared to be. The tears and stains of the old newspaper obscured the image. The headline read, "Monster Hoax on Local Hunter's Property."

Kay started reading. The article was about Jonny Langley. It described how Jonny went missing on Dee's property— something Kay already knew—and that the townspeople found a melted gun and large, bird-like footprints— something Kay did not know. "You're fucking kidding me," Kay said aloud to Shotgun. She continued reading.

Apparently, Jonny showed up three days after going missing. Then, a few days later, the Bennett Boys admitted to setting up the elaborate hoax.

Kay couldn't get past the melted metal and bird feet. "Talk to Jonny Langley," she scribbled on a notepad she had shoved in her backpack.

There wasn't any more information in the article, and Kay couldn't find any more articles about that incident.

After another hour of scouring the internet, Kay still had little to no answers.

Kay couldn't hold it together anymore. She hugged her knees tightly to her chest. The tears came fast and hard. Her whole body shook with the weight of it all; messy, hiccupping sobs echoed in the quiet cabin.

What was she doing? She had no career, no money, and now she thought she had some kind of magical power? Was it possible for her OCD to have consumed her? Maybe she had finally cracked, and what she thought was a power was really intrusive visual thoughts taking over her brain. She had just spent an hour on the internet reading message boards about missing time, acid trips, and spiritual journeys hoping to find some answers.

Shotgun sat right beside her, calm and steady. He didn't try to lick her face or nudge her to get up. He just stayed there, close, leaning his warm head against her leg.

Chapter 14

11:47 a.m. – "Let's take you out," Kay told Shotgun as he danced next to the front door, his bone now bits of wet marrow soaking into the sterile couch. She had cried all the tears that she could muster and felt relieved—the way you do after a good cry.

They stood at the bottom stair of the front porch, staring at each other.

"Go ahead." Shotgun didn't move. He had been acting strangely all morning. Normally, he loved being at Dee's property and took off running into the woods the second he could. Not today.

Finally, after a lot of encouragement, he went to the bathroom about fifteen yards from the front door, then sprinted right back to Kay's side. He was oddly glued to her.

As they walked back into the cabin, Kay's phone buzzed.

"Any luck getting that big one?"

It was a text from Nick Knight. They didn't text often, but when they did, it was always about bowhunting.

"No dice," Kay texted back.

She contemplated telling Nick about her whole bizarre morning. She was shocked at herself about how mellow and stoic she was acting. Being at Dee's cabin, without all the people around, was peaceful, so maybe it was a false sense of calm she was feeling.

She picked up her backpack and walked to the adjoining, small bathroom across the living room.

The bathroom was the one part of the cabin that the realtor hadn't ruined. The baby-blue toilet and matching tiles on the walls looked like a feature photo from a 1970s home interiors magazine. The bathroom was a time warp and Kay's favorite part of the cabin.

She placed her open backpack next to the claw-foot tub and began to undress. Kay figured a warm shower would help her get her head straight. As she pulled off her T-shirt, she winced.

"Damn, my shoulder." In all the craziness, she had forgotten that she hurt her left shoulder in her fall from the treestand, and now it screamed at even the slightest touch.

With her shirt off, she turned to examine her shoulder in the vintage, gold-rimmed oval mirror.

Kay leaned over the baby-blue porcelain sink to get a better look.

"Shit…" she whimpered.

Her shoulder wasn't bruised, it wasn't cut. Instead, she found a large, circular welt, about three inches in diameter. The welt was just above her black-silhouette Abbey Road tattoo. The skin was raised, red, and very swollen. Kay almost thought that she saw a pattern—spiral-like—in the swelling.

Kay leaned in even closer and lightly touched the welt. The touch sent a shockwave of pain through her body. She rummaged through the cabinet behind the mirror and found some BlackHole-brand painkillers. Kay popped two in her mouth, finished undressing, and stepped into the warm water.

She clung to the wolf necklace around her neck. "Man, Penny, I wish you were here right now to make me laugh about all of this."

Kay sat next to Shotgun on the stiff couch cushions, dry, clean, and in fresh clothes. She needed help and, for whatever reason, Nick Knight was the only person she trusted. Kay pulled out her phone and sent a text.

"Do you remember where my grandmother's property is?"

A few long minutes later, "Yes, I do!" Nick responded.

"Can you meet me there in an hour?"

Her phone buzzed. "Sure, is this about that big eight-point?"

"Kind of… See you in a few."

And with that, she hugged Shotgun and waited patiently.

90

Chapter 15

Kay heard Nick's red-and-white 1980s rebuilt Ford Bronco roll up the gravel driveway toward the cabin. She loved that truck.

She got up from the couch where she and Shotgun had started to fall asleep.

Kay's heart was pounding, not with panic this time, but excitement. She had known Nick almost her entire life, and her chest still fluttered every time she saw him.

Nick's leather work boots crunched on the gravel as he stepped out of the driver's side. His red and black plaid flannel was tucked meticulously into his tight blue jeans. His rugged manliness was always combined with impeccable presentation. Nick pulled off his black aviator sunglasses and lightheartedly asked, "So, where is this monster deer I'm helping you drag?"

"Yeah… About that… There's no deer at all. Not even a doe."

"Oh, okay! Well, I'm happy to see you," Nick answered as he hugged Kay. She breathed in his faint teakwood cologne. He was never shy about touching Kay. He was never shy at all. Kay thought that was what she liked most about Nick. He was very honest about himself and his intentions.

Kay, on the other hand, was guarded and wary. She never touched anyone. Hugging her own mother was awkward. Since being internet-bullied and since BlackHole stole her art, she had become even more distrusting and robotic in her interactions. Warmth was a social tool Kay used to gain other people's trust, but warmth never came naturally to her.

Nick let go. Kay was flustered. What was it about this guy that made her so disoriented and trusting at the same time?

He followed her inside.

"Oh wow, the realtor really changed things up in here…" he complimented with a tone of sarcasm.

"Yeah, it's awful," Kay confirmed. Nick had visited this cabin a few times before. Dee used to host huge archery opening day parties with a welcoming breakfast spread and freshly ground coffee. She would invite local hunters to use her property throughout the season, and, of course, Marcus Knight, Nick's dad, was at the top of Dee's list. Dee always admired and respected first responders, and Marcus was the king of cops in Owlsbourne.

Nick sat on the couch, then cringed in discomfort. "What is it with couches like this?"

"I know. So stupid," Kay agreed, distracted, as she picked up her laptop and sat on the rug next to Shotgun.

"So, remember the bear I told you about yesterday?" she asked.

"Yes," Nick answered. The sunlight broke through the window, highlighting all his best features.

"I don't know what is going on with me, and I am going to sound insane telling you this. I also don't know why I am telling you all of this," Kay said hesitantly.

"Well, geez, I'm flattered," Nick laughed.

Her heart rushed.

She breathed, "So that bear looked really weird. My initial thought was that it was not a bear. And honestly, I should have trusted my gut. I've been in the woods long enough to know what I'm looking at. I know that sounds weird, and you can leave if you want before I take you down this rabbit hole. I just didn't know who else to call."

Nick nudged himself off the couch a bit, moving closer to Kay. He wasn't going anywhere, and Kay knew that. He was steady and rational, and at that moment, she was so thankful for him.

"That doesn't sound weird at all. Who knows what is in the woods, honestly? Never mind the ocean! We've only discovered a fraction of the species on Earth. I know you saw whatever it is you think you saw. You're one of the best hunters that I know. You know these woods like the back of your hand," Nick comforted her as he placed his hand on her shoulder.

"Right," Kay answered, not noticing Nick flirting with her, "So… whatever it was didn't even look like it was from this planet. You know? I know how that sounds."

"Okay, describe it," Nick suggested calmly.

"The creature was all black with an oversized, slightly oval head and big, black, scary eyes. There was no fur at all. It was skinny. That's why I originally thought maybe mange or a disease. Probably about seven feet tall, standing. Also, it seemed like weightless..? It was just balancing on a pine branch. I couldn't see everything. It was far away, about 100 yards, and obscured by branches. It had some red mark on its chest. I couldn't see a mouth or nose, only eyes. Its fingers kind of resembled talons…? But again, it was all obscured and blurry," her heart was beating out of her chest.

Nick didn't flinch. "Okay, then what?"

"Well, then, I got down from my treestand, ran to my car, and drove to work. I tried not to think about it. But then the whole thing gets stranger. That's why now I think the creature had something to do with everything." In that moment, Shotgun dropped a tennis ball at Kay's feet. Nick grabbed the ball and tossed it across the room for Shotgun to chase.

"Go on," her said to Kay, his eyes were soft and understanding.

"Don't tell anyone this, okay?" Kay pressed.

"You have my word," Nick reassured.

This morning, I went back out hunting. This time, I took the bear spray and sat in the willow tree. Do you know the treestand in the corner of the property near the junkyard? Yesterday, I sat in the oak tree on the other side of the property.

"Yeah, I got you," Kay could see that Nick was mapping out the treestands on the property in his mind. He was familiar enough to know what she was talking about.

"Well, this morning I was sitting in the willow tree and, before the sun came up, I saw a huge flash of white light, then I woke up on the ground a few hours later. It was terrifying," all the details were flooding out of her. "I assumed I fell asleep, that my safety harness had snapped, and I had fallen out of the treestand. Except when I climbed back up, my carabiner had melted. Here, look," Kay grabbed her phone and pulled up the photos she had taken of the scene earlier.

"Whoa," was all Nick mustered as he stared at the images in disbelief.

Kay added, "I didn't break any bones and feel fine."

"Another thing to note is that I found an article this morning about Jonny Langley. They found his gun melted here in 1989. Supposedly, it was a hoax. But I think it would be worth talking to him."

Kay continued without waiting for Nick's reaction, "Now this is when I start to sound really unhinged. I know I'm an artist and weird and don't have a ton of friends, so maybe it sounds like I'm making this up," Kay demeaned herself, trying to beat Nick to the punch.

"Kay, stop. You are so far from unhinged and weird. You are talented and the smartest, hardest-working person I know. I trust what you say," Nick firmly interjected.

Nick had always supported Kay and her art. He bought her largest, most expensive prints when she was selling art prints and trying to make it big. One of those prints is still hanging on the front wall of Shadowflight Archery.

"Thank you," she responded shyly. Nick tossed the ball again for Shotgun.

"I also have this welt on my shoulder. I think I fell on it. I don't know. It's just another odd thing."

Kay paused.

"Well, that isn't *that* strange," Nick looked confused.

"No, this is the really bizarre part. Please don't think I'm insane."

"I promise I will not think you're insane," Nick reassured Kay again.

She paused and took a breath.

"When I was driving here this morning, after falling out of the treestand, I think I saw into other people's minds..." she stammered.

"Like not inside their brains, but every time I blinked, I could see through their eyes. I could see their perspective. I even think I was feeling the emotions they were feeling..."

Kay looked at Nick for reassurance, but this time, he just sat with a blank stare. Shotgun nudged his foot, but Nick didn't budge.

She closed her eyes, hesitated momentarily, and continued, "I saw the perspectives of a criminal and a cop. At first, I thought, well, that's just weird and not real. I figured I was tired and just imagining things in my head. But then, when I got to my apartment building, I saw through my little neighbor's perspective and witnessed her mom abusing her. What I saw in my mind was something that I would never imagine. So, my gut reaction was to call 911," Kay stopped as she heard herself talk. *What the fuck?* Hearing her own words, she knew she sounded like a maniac.

"The cops showed up and ended up taking the girl's mom away in handcuffs because she was keeping the girl trapped in a closet. Exactly what I saw in my mind minutes before the police arrived."

The room started spinning, then the whole world started spinning. Kay's stomach turned. She squeezed her eyes shut. She was panicking again.

"Don't let Nick think you're crazier than you already sound." The stress of the morning was overwhelming. Why would she tell the only guy that she had ever really had a crush on that... essentially, she was having a mental breakdown? Maybe because she was having a mental breakdown...

"Okay… Give me a second to process this. Maybe there's a reasonable explanation. My intuition is spot on sometimes, too," Nick rationalized.

Now Kay was defensive, "No. It was not intuition. I know intuition. This was terrifying. I saw through other people's eyes, I know it."

Then she blinked. Suddenly, Kay saw herself sitting on a dusty, mauve rug. She appeared messy, scared, and pleading. Her face was tired and desperate. She looked down and saw a red and black flannel, tight blue jeans, and Shotgun.

She opened her eyes.

"How do you feel right now?" She asked Nick.

"Well, I'm kind of freaking out," he answered honestly.

"I believe what you're saying. But this is a lot. Like, it's a little strange."

"The situation is strange, not you," he immediately corrected himself.

"My theory, which I think you just confirmed, is that the visions only seem to happen when someone is in a heightened state of stress or discomfort. Also, my proximity to people seems to matter."

She was talking so matter-of-factly. How was she okay with this? Maybe because, for the first time in years, she felt excited. The fire in her, she assumed was snuffed out by doubt and despair, had suddenly sparked to life by these bizarre new experiences. There was a blaze inside her she so desperately missed.

"How did I confirm that?" Nick asked skeptically.

"When I blinked, I saw your perspective," Kay answered calmly.

"But you blinked for, like, not even a second," Nick was perplexed.

"That part doesn't make sense either. I stay in the visions for what seems like minutes, but I don't seem to lose much time in the physical world. Maybe I'm getting a glimpse of the future? I don't know. Or a glimpse of time as a web, and not linear." She didn't even know what she was talking about. She had heard about the time thing on the Science Channel late at night.

"Okay. I'm going to go with all of this for a second," Nick agreed hesitantly, "How can you prove and refine this… ability?"

He wasn't mocking her or taunting in any way; Nick was genuinely asking.

"Well, I have some ideas, but I'm extremely nervous to be around people because… either this is real and I need to figure it out, or I honestly need to commit myself," Kay admitted seriously. She had thought a lot about the implications of everything she was claiming and everything she had experienced in the last forty-eight hours.

"One idea that I had was to go to The Golden Sphinx and try playing poker," The Golden Sphinx was the seedy casino in East Owlsbourne, "I figure that there are a lot of stressed people at casinos and poker is the perfect game to know if I'm seeing other people's perspectives instantly."

"Okay… Isn't that cheating, though? I mean, if you can "see" their hand. Plus, I haven't been back to The Golden Sphinx since I got in trouble years ago. I try to avoid that place completely," Nick pushed back. Shotgun had given up on trying to play and was back to gnawing his bone on the couch.

"Yeah, I guess you're right. I thought it'd just be a quick way to test my theories," Kay said quietly and manipulatively. She really wanted to go to The Golden Sphinx, and she knew Nick would eventually cave.

Kay was being selfish. But what was the harm in embracing this weird power, if it existed? She needed to figure it out. Plus, a little money in her pocket would be an inconceivable relief, since she was broke. She would never confess that part to Nick, of course.

"We can just go for an hour, two hours tops," Kay pressed. She didn't even recognize this confident, assertive version of herself.

Nick thought for a moment, "What the hell? Let's do it. This is all so surreal, anyway."

Kay jumped up from the ground and hugged him.

"Thank you for entertaining this and not bailing on me," her heart raced. This time, she touched him first.

"I trust you. You should trust yourself more," he encouraged kindly, as he held both of her hands and looked straight into her eyes. He never backed down from anything.

"Let's go to that creepy casino," he laughed as he stood up to leave.

Before leaving the property, Kay took Nick to the treestand where she had fallen. She showed him the melted carabiner, but aside from that, they couldn't find anything strange or out of place in the area.

Then, they locked Shotgun in the cabin and headed out toward the casino.

Chapter 16

2:28 p.m. – The Golden Sphinx was under a highway bypass in East Owlsbourne. Next door was a QuikCash lender storefront and a hole-in-the-wall Chinese restaurant. It was commonplace for the gamblers to grab cash and some egg rolls, then head into the casino for the day—or days.

The Golden Sphinx was past its prime. The exterior resembled a rundown, beige 1980s warehouse that could use a good power washing. Its neon blue and red dice lights flickered in the sun. Burned-out parts of the dice made the sign look like two empty neon cubes.

Behind the casino sprawled a forgotten construction site. Work had begun years ago on a grand expansion, but the project stalled and slowly decayed into permanence. Now, two rusting, BlackHole-branded cranes loomed overhead, frozen mid-task. The back lot of The Golden Sphinx property was nothing more than a vast pit of dirt now.

Inside the casino, the air was thick with cigarette smoke and broken dreams. The red and gold carpeting had seen better days, and the yellowing ceiling tiles looked ready to cave in at any moment. The mechanical rings and dings of slot machines echoed through the noisy atmosphere.

Patrons huddled around sticky card tables. Drained and worn, the dealers robotically shuffled cards. Dim lighting masked the stains on the walls and carpets from forgotten spills and negligence.

Each motley character seemed to have a tragic story etched into his or her face.

Over the casino loudspeaker, Kay heard, "Hi folks! Siren Hex speaking. You know me as the president of BlackHole, but did you also know that Thanksgiving is my and my daughter's favorite holiday? What—" That ad was getting very annoying.

BlackHole bought The Golden Sphinx a few years ago with plans to revitalize it. The place was still a dump, but now it screamed BlackHole everywhere. There were signs for BlackHole credit cards, BlackHole-branded cocktails, and more. The advertising was endless.

While Kay took in the entire scene, Nick greeted casino employees like long-lost family, hugging and laughing. They gave him free drinks and tokens and showed him photos of their kids. Did he know all these people from high school when he was arrested? Kay wanted to figure out Nick's relationship with these people more, but she couldn't focus right now.

Kay was right. This was a place full of stress, despair, and heightened emotions. Every time she blinked, she saw something new in her mind—like a movie playing in the back of her brain. The visions affirmed to her that this power, or whatever it was, was not made up. Everything she saw in her mind correlated with something happening in the physical world.

Kay could barely take a step without being overcome with mental visuals and deep emotions. She would open her eyes, and the room would spin. She would close her eyes and see foreign scenes from around the casino.

She blinked and saw clammy hands holding a cheap vodka soda in the left and a cell phone in the right, with a text that read, "Come home. We do not have the money, Tim. I can't pick up any more shifts. Please stop this, or I will have to take the kids to my sister's place."

She opened her eyes. "Shit," she said aloud.

Kay blinked again. This time, she saw an elderly woman's hand inserting coins into a slot machine. "Just one more pull," she heard.

She opened her eyes again.

It was too much.

Nick's voice was distant. He asked Kay how she felt, but she couldn't articulate anything. She thought she might faint.

"Sorry, one second," Kay blurted out and bolted toward the women's bathroom sign up ahead.

Kay clutched the toilet in the handicap stall as she revisited the Pop-Tart from that morning.

At the bathroom sink, she splashed some water on her face and pulled a stick of gum out of her pocket.

"Get it together. You're just going crazy," she laughed under her breath, in a deranged kind of way. This was all too insane.

Once she collected herself, she left the bathroom to meet Nick. Nick and Kay found an open poker game and headed to the ATM.

Nick pulled her aside. "Here, start with this." Nick handed Kay $350 in cash.

She was shocked. "Nick, no way! Keep that."

Kay was going to take the chance of being late on her bills and gamble any cash she had in her bank account. She would rather do that than admit to Nick that she was broke.

"No, seriously. Just take it. I am excited to see you lose it when your 'magical power' disappears at that table," he teased and gestured toward the Allerzil-branded poker table.

"Plus, I've been working overtime at Shadowflight. I would love to gamble some of the extra cash, but I'm on the straight and narrow now," he winked, "so you can gamble it for me."

Kay smiled. "Fine. But I'm getting you all of it back, plus some."

"Famous last words. That should be the slogan of this godforsaken place," Nick laughed as he gently touched her lower back and nudged her toward the table.
"Go on, killer."

Kay took a seat at the Texas Hold'em poker table, while Nick found a spot at a slot machine within earshot.

She had played poker a few times with Dee at Dee's parties, but Kay was no card shark.

Breathe… She was still seeing random scenes in her mind every time she shut her eyes. *Focus.*

Kay figured she wasn't totally freaking out over this "power" because she didn't want to embarrass herself (more than she already had) in front of Nick.

The air was thick with anticipation. Seated at the green felt table were three other individuals and Kay.

The dealer shuffled the cards, his hands moving with precision.

Under the flickering light, to the left of Kay, sat a middle-aged woman with auburn hair and a poker face, nonchalantly sipping her cosmopolitan as she studied her hand.

Beside that lady was a squirrely, strung-out-looking twenty-something man with greasy blonde hair and freehanded tattoos, nervously tapping his fingers on the edge of his cards.

To Kay's right was an elderly woman in a wheelchair with snow-white hair and skin. She grinned mischievously as soon as she saw her hand.

The tension in the room grew as the first round of betting commenced.

Bets were placed and chips exchanged hands.

Kay blinked.

Chapter 17

According to her theory, Kay would only see another player's hand if the player was stressed. It was important to note that she couldn't control the other person's actions or hear their inner thoughts. She could only see their perspective, hear and feel the physical world, and feel their emotions.

Just as Kay predicted, these players were anxious, especially as the game's stakes grew higher. As she blinked, she could see every player's hand. Her opponents were all nervous.

What Kay hadn't quite mastered was being able to manipulate whose perspective she was seeing in her mind—and when. She was just seeing random scenes. But proximity seemed to be the most significant factor in whose perspective she saw first.

The visions were like channels on a television in her brain.

By the flop, the squirrely guy had folded. By the turn, the auburn-haired lady had folded. That lady was actually dealt a better hand than Kay.

By the river, it was just Kay and the elderly woman in a face-off. When Kay blinked, she saw the woman's white hands shaking, holding a losing hand. Kay felt, through the woman's eyes, the woman's overwhelming discomfort and a deep sorrow. *What is this lady's story?* Kay couldn't help but wonder.

Kay was getting distracted. *Focus!* she yelled at herself in her mind.

Then, the players revealed their cards. Kay won.

She glanced over at Nick, across the room, who raised his eyebrows in surprise. Then he texted her from over at the slot machine, "Maybe just a fluke? You gotta hone in this power, Kay McQuinn!"

Kay and the elderly woman stayed at the table. A new cast of players joined them.

Again, Kay won.

Nick texted her again. "Maybe one more? Don't want to look sketchy."

Kay had $850 of chips stacked in front of her right now. "Okay," she texted back.

Her mind was still whirring, but as she sat in the chaos of the casino, she started to settle into the "power." The visions were less jumbled, less uncontrollable, and less suffocating. It was almost as if her mind responded to her heart rate and overall composure. The calmer she was, the less intense the power felt.

As she leaned into her discomfort, her discomfort dissipated.

Kay felt a strange peace while using the power—almost like she was meditating.

The dealer was interested now. His sleepy eyes came alive as he sized up Kay. A few local patrons had gathered around the Allerzil poker table to watch the spectacle. Murmurs buzzed from the onlookers.

One more game.

Kay played; this time, she was calmer, more controlled, less erratic feeling—and she won.

She stood up from the table.

The audience, disappointed, booed and encouraged her to play another round.

"That's it. I'm going to tap before I start getting unlucky," she announced to the crowd as she gathered her chips.

Kay walked over to Nick at the slot machine.

Nick's normally composed demeanor was gone, replaced by a mixture of bewilderment and awe. His brows furrowed. "What the hell was all that? All right, Kay

McQuinn, I think I believe you. Not that I didn't before…
but now I'm just… shocked."

"Can you stop calling me by my full name?" Kay laughed
as a few of her chips fell to the ground. She had won too
many chips to hold.

"Let me get that for you, m'lady." Nick bent down to pick
up the runaway chips.

He continued, "Sorry for using your full name, I just feel
like I'm with a celebrity. I mean, I always feel that way
when I'm with you," his cheeks flushed, "but I've never
seen Vinny so interested in a game. He's like the laziest,
most uninterested employee here."

"Who is Vinny?" Kay asked.

Nick gestured toward the *Sopranos* cast member dealer
who had just run the games she won.

"How do you know all these people?" Kay blurted out.

Nick clammed up, and he crossed his arms. "I told you, I
came here a lot when I used to get in trouble way back in
the day. That's in the past. Let's go cash in these chips, rich
girl."

There was something so suspicious about Nick's
relationship with The Golden Sphinx, but Kay hadn't quite
figured out what that something was.

Chapter 18

Kay and Nick walked over to the cashier's cage and cashed out Kay's chips. She had made $1,250. That would float her for the month! And, of course, she would pay Nick back.

Kay wanted to feel happy, but won money always felt like dirty money.

While she shoved the cash in her wallet quickly so no wandering eyes would see it, Kay spotted her poker opponent. The old woman from the poker table was rolling her wheelchair over to a *Mega Moolah* slot machine.

Kay's visions hadn't stopped. When she blinked, she saw unrecognizable scenes over and over again. She wasn't being stoic or cavalier about it; instead, she was sort of numb. She just wanted to get out of The Golden Sphinx.

"Hang on," Kay said to Nick as she took off walking toward the old woman.

There was something so somber about this lady. Kay couldn't shake the emotion she felt when looking through the old lady's eyes.

"Excuse me, ma'am." Kay tapped the woman's shoulder just as the woman was about to pull the *Mega Moolah* lever.

The old woman turned her wheelchair to face Kay. Her eyes were distant. The weight of time pulled at the corners of her eyes. Sadness draped across her face, painting a poignant portrait of a woman who had weathered many of life's storms. Her white hair framed her round features. Her makeup reminded Kay of Jane in *What Ever Happened to Baby Jane?* It was cakey, white, and cracking—a failed attempt at looking youthful. Her pink lipstick softened the harsh creases in her makeup.

"I wanted to give you this," Kay said, handing the woman $900.

The woman looked shocked. Before she could say a word, tears began rolling down her cheeks, streaking her pasty foundation.

"No, no, I can't take that from you." The woman's voice was raspy and low from years of smoking. Her frail hand pushed the money back toward Kay.

"Please. I'll win other games," Kay said, opening the woman's hand and placing the cash in her palm.

Before the woman could respond, Kay turned away and walked back toward Nick. She didn't need to know the details of this woman's story to understand that the lady was in pain.

Suddenly, everything was too much. Kay was feeling it all, seeing it all. She needed to get back to the woods—away from people.

She walked right past Nick toward the neon red exit sign. He jogged to catch up.

Kay slammed herself into the push bar on the heavy metal door and tumbled outside into the daylight. The sun felt warm and inviting on her cigarette- smoke–drenched hair and skin, and the cool autumn air washed over her.

Kay lifted her hands to cover her face as she began to sob, right in the middle of The Golden Sphinx parking lot.

Chapter 19

The exterior door to The Golden Sphinx slammed shut behind Kay as Nick's strong arms embraced her. Kay wept on his chest.

Kay was panicking. She was depressed; she was confused; she was feeling all of it in that moment. She closed her eyes and got flashes of foreign scenes and emotions on the screen in the back of her mind. Her brain spun like a toppling top, entirely out of control.

Was she insane? What was happening? What was that creature she saw?

The warmth of Nick's body pressed against hers created a haven of comfort.

"You are safe," he whispered to her.

"Breathe," he repeated, again and again.

She could feel Nick's steady heartbeat—a rhythmic reassurance that echoed through his chest. They had an unspoken understanding—they always had—but in that moment, it was loud and clear. Two small-town kids, familiar with the dark side of life, ready to fight the whole world. She breathed in his teakwood-scented cologne, her makeup smeared into the flannel fibers of his shirt.

"This is too much. I'm crazy. I can't do this. Like, I don't even understand myself. I don't know what is going on. I'm a fucking loser," she blubbered through her tears. "I can't do anything right. Now, this morning, I go and fall out of a tree? *I guess*? And now I think I have a superpower? *And* I call you?!" She scoffed, not caring who heard.

Nick pulled away from her. He had frustration in his eyes now. He grabbed both her shoulders, pushed her to arm's length, lifted her chin, and looked Kay straight in the eyes.

"That's enough—no pity parties for Kay McQuinn. You are not a loser. You are the opposite of a loser. You are the most successful person I know and an incredibly talented artist. I know that maybe, on the day-to-day, it might not feel that way. I get it. But do you know how many people would love to be you? A hot, smart, healthy, famous artist? Stop this bullshit talk. I know that this power, or whatever, seems scary, and that makes sense. Your feelings are valid. But I won't sit by and let you talk shit about yourself. I am here with you. We will figure this out. I'm not going anywhere."

Then, he hugged her again. This time, firmer—like he was trying to squeeze the unhappiness out of her. No one had ever spoken to her like that before—so direct, so affirming.

"Let's get back to Shotgun," he insisted as he walked toward the Bronco.

Kay, disheveled and left standing alone in the parking lot, wiped her wet face and pushed the sticky strands of hair behind her ears. She chased after him.

"Whoa, okay, okay, no pity party," she relented with her hands up in surrender.

Nick didn't hear her; he was already jumping into the driver's seat.

Kay ran around the truck to the passenger door and got in.

"Thank you," was all she could think to say.

"Don't thank me. I mean everything that I say," Nick answered as he peered in the rearview mirror and shifted into reverse.

"Oh, hang on," Kay said as she pulled the remaining $350 of her winnings out of her wallet. "Here you go," she said as she stuffed the cash into the cupholder between them. "Thank you for letting me borrow that."

"No, I don't want that back. You proved me wrong and won every game," Nick asserted.

"Absolutely not, you take it," Kay insisted.

"Kay, I want you to keep it," Nick said firmly.

"Thank you, but no," Kay maintained. "How about this? You can treat us to a pizza from Frankie's on our way back to the cabin." She was starving after vomiting in the bathroom earlier.

"Deal," Nick relented and smiled. "Pepperoni?"

"Duh," Kay answered. "I'll call it in."

Chapter 20

5:27 p.m. – Coincidentally (or not), Jonny Langley worked at Frankie's Pizzeria part-time. He was a busboy, and Kay secretly hoped he would be on shift when she suggested picking up the pizza to Nick.

It was dark by the time Kay and Nick pulled into the parking lot at Frankie's. The incoming winter season had made the days unbearably short.

A hand-painted sign above the door, slightly faded from time, read *Frankie's Pizzeria* in red script. A string of twinkling lights hung lazily around the perimeter of the red-striped awning, glowing faintly in the nighttime haze.

Kay could smell the baking dough, tangy tomato sauce, and garlic wafting out of the ajar front door as she stepped out of the Bronco. A bell above the door jingled with every customer who came and went.

Kay immediately tried to peer into the shop but couldn't see Jonny. He must not have been working—*darn it*.

"What are you looking for?" Nick asked.

"Nothi—" Just as Kay was answering him, she spotted Jonny dragging a large black bag of trash to the dumpster on the side of the building.

"Hang on." Kay left Nick's side and ran over to Jonny. She wrapped herself in her arms, trying to fend off the brisk November air, and squeezed the wolf pendant hanging around her neck.

Jonny was in his late fifties. He was tall and wiry, with the kind of gauntness that made his cheekbones sharp and his eyes sink just enough to give them a hollow, wolfish look. His long, dark, gray-streaked hair was pulled back into a greasy ponytail. He had a thick, grizzled beard. He wore dark, flour-caked jeans, a faded Frankie's T-shirt, and scuffed black leather boots. Jonny spoke in short, clipped sentences when he had to, which was rare. Aside from working, he only ever came into town for the essentials—coffee, canned goods, batteries—and always at odd hours.

People in town whispered about Jonny. Kay had heard that he used to be funny, kind, and involved in the community. That certainly wasn't the Jonny she knew. Honestly, she was a little nervous to approach him. He was the town's loner. People didn't get close to Jonny.

"Hey, Jonny!" Kay waved him down as he closed the lid to the dumpster.

Standing in front of him, she asked, "Can I ask you a question?"

He stared at her blankly. The cigarette hanging from his lips dripped ash onto the concrete.

"What?" He did not want to talk to her—that was obvious.

"Um, you know that hoax or whatever happened on my grandma's property in 1989? Could you tell me more about that day?" Kay questioned, shakily.

Jonny shifted. The question made him uncomfortable. His eyes darted around, looking for an escape.

He didn't look directly at Kay. "I don't know anything about that. Why don't you go ask those Bennett boys what happened?"

He suggested it with a softness—almost embarrassment—that Kay was not expecting.

Now, Nick was standing next to Kay, listening intently to the conversation.

"Well, I don't think they can help me. I don't know. I just have a feeling that something happened to you out there," Kay suggested.

Jonny shifted again. "You've heard the story—it was a hoax."

He was eyeing the pizza shop over Kay's shoulder, hoping to get back to work as he started picking at a loose string on his jeans.

"Well, I don't know. Something weird happened to me out there this morning. I don't remember exactly everything, but my carabiner melted into a tree. And I think I saw a—" she hesitated "—creature on that land yesterday."

There was a momentary spark in Jonny's eyes when Kay said *creature*. Kay continued, "I read about your gun melting, and I just can't figure out how or why those dumb Bennett boys would do that."

Jonny shrugged. "They're bullies. It was just a prank."

Kay could tell he wasn't giving up any information. She thought she'd make one more plea.

"I'd really appreciate any help. Can we just sit and talk for a minute? Weird stuff has been happening to me since earlier today…" Kay pleaded.

Jonny stared at her. He looked like he might be thinking… or he just wanted her to leave. Kay wasn't sure.

"Okay. Well, if you change your mind, here's my number." Kay had scribbled her number onto a cocktail napkin from The Golden Sphinx.

Jonny took it and nodded.

Kay and Nick turned to leave when suddenly Jonny spit out, in a hushed voice,

"They're called the Umbravue."

Chapter 21

The three of them sat down around a wobbly metal table on the sidewalk in front of Frankie's.

Kay had suggested they sit down after Jonny agreed to talk for a minute.

Nick stayed quiet, observing. He felt protective of Kay.

"So what are… the Umbravue?" Kay asked. She imitated Jonny's pronunciation—"Um-brah-vooo."

Jonny looked down at the tabletop and pushed some crumbs around while he spoke.

"I'm not entirely sure," he answered shyly. "Honestly, it seems like a lot of the information about them has been scrubbed off the internet—or maybe it was never there in the first place.

"I've found some old books on lore in this area, and from what I've gathered, they're descendants of—or associated with—owls. They seem to be a very private species and only reveal themselves and their capabilities to chosen people—marked ones.

"Native Americans called them the Umbravue… I read that somewhere years ago. It means something like 'to see through darkness or shadows.'"

Kay was following… kind of. "Well, what about the melted metal?"

"Their powers seem to give off some intense heat signature. I haven't figured everything out. I've just strung together small bits of information from different books I've read.

"Here's what I'm pretty sure of—they're good. They want to spread goodness. They are extremely secretive. They have owl-like tendencies and behaviors. They have black skin, no feathers, and a red arrow spiral mark on their chests. They might be from another planet. They don't speak—they hum. Their feet and hands are large talons. They make you feel healed. It's not like they heal you; they kind of heal your soul. Does that make sense? Like they can make you feel okay and at peace. I've even read that they impart special powers to people—but I never personally experienced that…" He paused for a moment and gathered his thoughts. Jonny had done a lot of research and was very enthusiastic about all of it.

Kay thought back to all the times over the last several hours when she thought she would freak out or panic but instead felt peaceful or calm. Was that the healing Jonny was referring to?

"I don't think I was supposed to see them that day back in 1989, in the woods. Actually, I'm sure I wasn't supposed to see them. I don't even remember the days after that. I don't remember the search party—none of it. Apparently, I acted weird when they found me… I just don't remember…" He trailed off, his eyes distant now.

Kay was beside herself. Jonny looked so earnest; whatever he was saying, she could tell that at least *he* believed it was true. She had so many questions. "Wait, then why would the Bennett boys take credit for that incident as a hoax?"

Jonny squirmed, visibly uncomfortable. "I don't know. Ask them. I mean, they never shy away from the spotlight. Maybe someone convinced them to do it. All I know is that since then, I've been considered the town crazy," he said, frustrated.

Jonny was much more normal than Kay had thought. He had a reputation for being a little… off.

Just then, the front door to Frankie's swung open.

"Jonny! What the hell are you doing out here? I have a bunch of dirty tables in here!"

It was Clint, the manager of Frankie's.

"Sorry, I'm coming in," Jonny answered.

"You better!" Then Clint slammed the front door.

Jonny stood up to leave, then looked back at Kay and Nick. "Look, I gotta go."

He paused. "For years I have searched for information about those creatures, about that land, but I've only been able to scrape together tidbits. That's all I've got. But if you need more information, you know where to find me."

He gestured toward the pizza shop, got up from his seat, and walked toward the front door.

He turned back one more time.

"Hey! One more thing. I think they fly."

Chapter 22

5:58 p.m. – Kay and Nick didn't say much on the car ride back to Dee's cabin. They were stunned from the day and mentally drifting in a pepperoni-scented cloud as Nick drove the windy roads back to Dee's.

As soon as they got back to the cabin, Kay ran into the bathroom to brush her teeth and remove as much casino stench as she could from her skin, hair, and clothes. Then Kay let Shotgun out to run—except he still stayed right by her side. So she walked around the yard with him as Nick carried the pizza inside and grabbed some plates from Dee's kitchen.

When Kay and Shotgun returned to the house, in the dimly lit living room, they saw a pizza picnic on the mauve rug and heard a fire crackling in the woodstove. The air was filled with the aroma of freshly fired pizza dough and burning ash.

"I figured, since that couch is the actual worst and the new fancy table looks too nice to eat off of, we could have a picnic," Nick announced with his arms wide open, gesturing to the picnic he had set up on the ground.

He had dug out an old candle, which was lit in the center of the rug. Around the candle were two old metal camping plates, a dusty bottle of wine, and some tin camping cups.

Next to the rug, on the wood floor, was another plate that Shotgun had already discovered.

"I tore the crusts off my slices so that Shotgun could join us," Nick grinned.

Shotgun was already chewing on the blackened New Haven–style pizza crusts.

Kay's heart fluttered. "Well, this looks awesome. Thank you." She mirrored Nick's enthusiasm as she sat down. Her mind was quiet now, in the woods, and she could play along with Nick's picnic without the distraction of the visions.

Nick joined her as they started scarfing down the delicious slices of heaven. Was he going to bring up Jonny Langley and the "Umbravue," or should she?

Their eyes met, and they instantly started laughing, their mouths full of pizza.

"What a day!" Nick chuckled.

"Like, are you a poker genius or a superhero?!" He laughed even more.

Kay felt so light. Everything was easy with Nick. She laughed. "Well, I'm definitely not good at poker. What about that 'Umbravue' story?" she asked with air quotes.

Nick looked up, and his expression became serious. "Look… you saw that creature; I didn't. So, I don't know anything for certain. But Jonny Langley is…" Nick searched for a nice word, "eccentric. He doesn't have the nickname Jonny Jitters for no reason. So maybe we look into what he's talking about, but I wouldn't put too much stake into his story."

Kay nodded in agreement. Still, Jonny's story was bothering her. Sure, he was known to be a little weird, but some things he said had striking similarities to her experience.

Kay decided to enjoy the moment and let the topic die. She would do research later, but for now, she enjoyed the silence in her mind.

She and Nick were both so hungry. They focused on their favorite pizza.

Shotgun had finished his crusts and was snoozing on the couch.

Once Nick finished a couple of slices, he looked up again. "So, what's the plan?"

Kay was still savoring the lightness of the moment. "I don't know. I didn't find anything online earlier about melted metal or lights in the sky, or anything. I did, however, find invitations to new age cults and hallucinogenics websites," she said. "I can try searching again with Jonny's story in mind. Maybe I'll get different results if I search 'Umbravue.' I'll probably try that in a bit."

"Sounds good," Nick said, then paused. "I think I should stay here tonight. I don't want you to be alone out in these woods. Maybe we can try more tests tomorrow and see if this is really a superpower. What do you think?"

He was always so confident and determined. Kay was surprised by his candor, but honestly, she didn't want to be alone in the woods all night.

"Yeah, that works," she answered, trying to be nonchalant as she took her last bite.

Something had been on her mind since earlier at the casino.

"Can I ask you something?"

"Shoot," Nick answered openly.

"I know you said you know those people at the casino from getting in trouble, but you seemed really close to them. Did you go there that often? I didn't know you were really into gambling," Kay asked delicately. She was trying not to sound judgmental.

Nick's gaze turned agitated as he crossed his arms and sat up. "Umm…" He was clearly thinking about what to say.

"Fuck it," he said out loud to himself.

"I don't really talk about this. But you've been so open with me today, and I don't know—I trust you," he said, leadingly.

"I'm sorry. I didn't mean to make you uncomfortable," Kay immediately retracted her question.

"No, it's okay. I should probably talk more about this stuff," he relented.

"Okay. Definitely don't feel like you have to tell me anything." She gently touched his thigh as they sat Indian-style on the rug with the grease-stained, empty pizza box between them.

He took a breath. "Yeah, I had a fake ID for a bit and gambled at The Golden Sphinx." Nick paused and sipped the ancient red wine they had pulled from the pantry. "But that's not why everyone knows me there. They know me because I was there almost daily, trying to pay my dad's debts or convince my dad to come home. But boy, did that guy have a temper…" Nick's eyes were distant and sad.

Kay jumped in, "Your dad wasn't a gambler, though, right? He was like the hero of Owlsbourne." She was genuinely confused. Marcus Knight, the sheriff, was the pride and protector of Owlsbourne.

"Oh, he was a gambler, all right. He was an absolute, degenerate, addicted gambler and a violent father. I know the town saw him as something great, but he was my family's monster. I sometimes think I lived with the devil himself." Nick paused and took another sip of his wine.

"He wasn't always that way. There was a time when he was warm. When I was a kid, he would take me fishing and bowhunting. He always had a temper, but we knew how to behave, and he managed to keep it in check. Then, one day, he started playing online poker right after becoming a deputy. He started taking pills to stay up late and pills for energy in the morning. He got involved with the wrong people. Eventually, he started going over to The Golden Sphinx. He played in some back-room game to protect his fake reputation. When he wasn't working, he was there. If anyone got suspicious, he just claimed he was patrolling the place. He was so mean that no one dared rat him out."

"My mom started selling her tortillas, enchiladas, and burritos in the morning down in East Owlsbourne before her shift at Bob's to make up for the money my dad was losing."

Kay had eaten Maria Knight's food many times and could attest that it was the best. Maria had immigrated to the United States from Mexico in the 1970s. That was all Kay knew about her. She was a petite woman with beautiful, black, curly hair and dark features. Maria had well-worn hands from working her entire life and a face that told a story. Kay saw Maria when Maria was working her shift at Bob's Corner Grocer, but they only spoke in formalities about the weather or a local football game. Their conversations had always been superficial. Still, Maria radiated warmth. Her kind eyes complemented her permanently upturned lips.

Shotgun was really snoring now, completely unaware that he was interrupting an intimate moment between Kay and Nick. Nick didn't notice and continued.

"My mom made ends meet for a while, but when she got sick, she couldn't work anymore. I know my dad cared about her, but there was this evil version of him that only emerged when he was gambling and drinking. He was Dr. Jekyll and Mr. Hyde. Owlsbourne got Dr. Jekyll, and my family got Mr. Hyde. My brother couldn't handle it. He took off to boarding school up in Massachusetts, leaving me to pick up the pieces."

Kay remembered when Maria was diagnosed with cancer. She and Nick were probably about twelve years old. The town held all kinds of fundraisers, and Marcus Knight was the poster boy for all of them.

Marcus Knight had always been widely respected and loved. Kay thought so highly of him. She couldn't imagine this Mr. Hyde that Nick was describing. But she could tell from the pain in Nick's eyes that he was very much—and very reluctantly—telling the truth.

"My dad started gambling away the fundraiser money that was supposed to pay for my mom's treatment. I didn't know what to do. So I started showing up at The Golden Sphinx to figure out exactly what was going on."

Nick looked like he might cry now. "What I found was so much worse than I thought. He was cheating on my mom, doing drugs, and had lost all our money. On top of that, he owed a lot of money to very bad people. I still don't know all his debts. But his debts went deep."

He continued, "I started going with my mom to her treatments. When she was in her appointments, I would ditch school and sell drugs, knock-off sneakers, whatever I could hustle to get money.

"My only priority was survival and getting money. Fuck. I didn't want my mom to die. She was the best thing in my life." His eyes welled with tears.

Kay scooted around the pizza box and put a hand on his back.

His body remained stiff, and he returned to his stoic demeanor, seemingly embarrassed that he had shown any emotion.

"Anyway, I did what I could for my mom, but the cancer ultimately won. I became the criminal of Owlsbourne—and actually, that title was accurate. I made bad decisions to survive, and I own that. My dad spiraled into a full-blown addiction after my mom's passing, and then he died in a car accident. The end," Nick spat with disdain. "No happily ever after, no big 'come to Jesus' moment—that was the big Hollywood finish. The story ended with both my parents dead, my brother gone, and me in a juvenile rehab program on meds that made me feel completely detached from the reality of it all."

Then Nick seemed to snap out of a trance and laughed. "And that is my big sob story, Kay McQuinn." He took the last sip of his wine. "I finally got my act together. I graduated, then Jimmy offered me a job at Shadowflight, and I've been working there ever since."

Kay stared at Nick's wine-stained lips, distracted. She listened intently. She was drawn to Nick and his vulnerability.

She had so many questions for him. His story added up the more she thought about it.

Right now, Kay didn't want to say anything. Instead, without thinking, she leaned in and kissed him in the soft glow of the wood-burning stove. Time stood still. It was a tender and cautious kiss. She tasted the cheap red wine as he kissed her back, harder and stronger.

Kay pulled away. "I'm so sorry." She was flustered. She hadn't forgotten about their bizarre day.

Now is not the time for this.

"Here you are telling me your life story, and I cut you off and do that." She tugged at the bottom hem of her T-shirt and looked down, away from Nick. Kay, desperate for a distraction, grabbed the bottle of wine and poured them each another glass. The tension hung in the air. "So sorry. I don't know why I did that. Please, please continue." She glanced back up at him.

This time, it was his lips that interrupted her words. His kiss was confident and excited. It felt charged with years of hidden lust. He pulled her close. Their bodies pressed together as they leaned against the bottom of the uncomfortable couch. Each touch was electrifying.

Kay wanted to keep going, but some part of her was wildly distracted by the overarching issue of her brain… malfunctioning, or whatever was happening.

She pulled away again. "I'm sorry. We probably shouldn't…" she declared, frazzled.

"I'm going to take Shotgun out one more time."

Before Nick could answer, Kay was out the cabin door, dog collar in hand, dragging Shotgun behind her.

Outside, in the brisk November air, Nick apologized.

"I'm really sorry," he said, his voice low and remorseful. "I didn't mean to get ahead of myself. I've never told anyone that stuff about my life—I guess I just got caught up in the moment. You know I like you. Or… I hope you know that. But you're right. Today's not the day. Not with everything going on. Just… please don't shut me out. I'm here. I mean that. We can figure this out. Together."

Kay's mind was as foggy as the evening air—not from any visions, but from pure emotions. At that moment, she didn't care about anything at all.

She didn't answer right away. But something about the way Nick looked at her—unguarded, steady, real—settled the storm inside her. For the first time in days, she felt both safe and seen. And somehow, that made her brave.

Kay spun around to Nick and delicately pushed herself against him. She kissed him—not slowly this time, but hard

and fast. Her lips clung to his with passion. This was a
romantic kiss, but not the beautiful, tender kind that sonnets
are written about. Instead, this was a provocative, messy,
wet kiss of desire.

Pressed against each other, not letting go, they clumsily
moved back toward the cabin.

Shotgun ran in under their feet as they crashed through the
front door.

Kay had already considered it: if her power was truly
induced by negativity and stress, then, according to her
theory, it shouldn't mess up this moment.

In the living room, Kay grabbed the cold, metal buckle of
Nick's leather belt, which had been holding up his tight
blue jeans all day. His strong fingers wove into her long,
shaggy hair, and he cradled her head against his mouth. She
pulled at the leather strap, undoing the buckle.

They continued kissing as she unbuttoned his perfectly
fitted shirt. Kay guided them toward the back bedroom.

They fell onto the new mid-century bed that the realtor had
neatly staged.

Kay, on top of Nick, ripped off her shirt while he pulled off
his flannel, revealing a dark, sculpted chest.

She began kissing him all over.

Chapter 23

Her theory was right—the power hadn't disrupted the moment. In fact, Kay felt better than she ever had. She was energized, clear-headed, healthy, and alive. She didn't know if it was the power or just being with Nick.

She wished she could talk to her best friend, Penny, and tell her she had hooked up with Nick Knight. Penny had teased her about having a crush on him throughout high school.

Kay rolled over; her shoulder still radiated pain from where the welt was. She looked at the gold analog clock on the nightstand.

9:56 p.m. – Nick traced his finger along her bare shoulder.

"What are you thinking? You didn't see into my brain or anything during that, right?" he asked, half-jokingly, as if that had not crossed his mind until now.

Kay rolled back over to face him. She laughed. "No, not at all. I definitely would have said something."

She took in the sparkle of his deep amber eyes. His dark hair clung, wet, to his forehead. Nick's head lay on the pillow as he stroked her arm with the tips of his fingers. Tiny beads of sweat rolled down his chest. Moonlight flooded through the window, turning the black of night into a magical glow.

"I'm just thinking that this all feels fucking crazy," Kay finally answered bluntly.

He shut his eyes. "I agree," he answered softly.

Then he opened his eyes. "Here is what I propose. Let's get a good night's sleep and try to conquer superpowers and aliens… or the Umbravue… in the morning." His eyes were slits, heavy with exhaustion.

"That sounds good," Kay whispered.

"Deal." He leaned in and gently kissed her forehead.

Kay lay on her back, staring at the ceiling, thinking about her life, the universe, the day—everything.

Nick was asleep in less than two minutes.

Kay drifted off not long after that.

Chapter 24

SUNDAY

7:02 a.m. – Her dreams were strange.

When Kay awoke, she did not feel like she had dreamed all night, but instead that she existed in another dimension. The dreams were tangible and emotional.

Her mind was already swirling. Should she tell Nick about the dreams? She was trying to play it cool with Nick, and with each new development in this strange experience, she worried she sounded crazier.

She closed her eyes, stretched her arms above her head, and took in the sunlight that washed over the bed. Her bare left shoulder was less tender than the night before. She craned her neck to look at it, but all she saw was a bit of redness— and the welt, which appeared more defined now. Instead of a welt, it almost looked like a brand.

Kay pulled the sheets over her naked chest, closed her eyes, and breathed in the sweet aroma of freshly brewed coffee.

Nick must be in the kitchen. Shotgun wasn't in the bedroom, either.

Kay dragged herself out of bed.

Her thoughts were clouded with a weird haze of elation, horror, and confusion. Did that really happen last night with Nick?

Did yesterday really happen? Was she really seeing into people's perspectives—into their minds, into their lives? It was all too much.

Kay willed herself not to panic or overthink.

Instead, she grabbed some fresh clothes and slipped into the bathroom. She noted, again, that she felt especially at peace and good, despite all the strangeness and distress over the last two days.

Kay pulled back the shower curtain to take a quick rinse and cleanse herself of the casino smoke, pizza musk, and strange occurrences from the previous day.

As she turned to step into the shower, she caught a glimpse of the welt on her left shoulder in the mirror.

"What the actual…" she uttered. She lightly touched the welt and leaned closer to the mirror. "What the hell?"

Kay opened the bathroom door. "Nick!"

This was not the romantic morning-after greeting she had imagined, but she was freaking out.

Nick came rushing to the bathroom from the kitchen. He had already showered and was back to his pristine, put-together appearance.

"Good morning, beauti—" His voice trailed off when he saw Kay's horrified expression.

Nick followed Kay's eyes toward her left shoulder. He instantly noticed a spiral brand on her skin. Nick stepped closer.

"Okay, let's just take a second," he reassured her in a shaky voice.

Kay had dropped her towel and was standing in the middle of the bathroom, naked, clutching her arm.

"Does that look like a brand to you?" she asked Nick, her words trembling.

"Um, yeah, it does," Nick answered matter-of-factly.

"Hang on, let me get closer." He brought his eyes about six inches above the welt. "It looks like a spiral with an arrow on the end, right?" he questioned, wide-eyed.

Kay looked back toward the mirror. She saw, reflected, her red, irritated skin in the shape of a spiral—with, yes, an arrow at the end.

"Nick, I'm freaking the fuck out. Didn't Jonny say something about 'marked ones'? And I haven't even told you about my dreams last night." She tried to hold it

together, but everything seemed surreal and connected—
while simultaneously feeling disconnected from her body
and this whole moment. Her brain couldn't process
everything.

"Okay," he cut her off, regaining his composure. "Breathe
for a second." He gently kissed the welt and pulled her bare
body in close.

"We'll talk about it all, but let's not get ahead of ourselves.
Stay present. Take a warm shower, and then we'll discuss
everything over fresh coffee. Today is our day to figure out
what the hell is going on. I am off work all weekend." He
gently rubbed her back to calm her. He was visibly
suppressing his own terrified emotions.

She answered him with a kiss. *I guess last night did
happen,* she thought as she slowly removed his perfectly
pressed clothing. She wanted a distraction.

They stepped into the shower together, their lips never
separating, as warm water cascaded over them.

Chapter 25

They each sipped their black coffee, hoping the caffeine would generate some profound revelation. Kay sat at the kitchen table, still clutching her arm. Shotgun lay in the morning sunlight on the floor, and Nick hummed "Vienna" by Billy Joel quietly as he fried some eggs and bacon for breakfast. The bacon sizzled and popped.

"Did you run to the store this morning, too?" Kay asked as she looked around the kitchen at the fruit, coffee, and dog food. "I didn't think Bob's was even open this early, especially on a Sunday."

"I know a guy," Nick winked. It seemed like he was always just a step ahead of her. He was suave and unwavering.

"Well, thank you," she said kindly as she took another sip of coffee.

"So, like, did I get abducted by aliens?" She laughed but was actually scared and thought she'd get straight to the point.

Nick laughed nervously as he cracked the eggs. "I honestly don't know. Tell me about these dreams that you had."

"Oh, yeah, right." She had forgotten about the dreams the second she spotted the giant spiral on her shoulder earlier.

She exhaled. How could she express this without sounding too insane?

"My dreams didn't feel like dreams. They felt like reality—but hazy, like reality with a glow. When I woke up, I felt like I lived inside the dream. It's hard to explain. I truly felt every emotion, and when I woke up, it just didn't feel like I had been sleeping."

She gave him a minute to absorb that as he flipped the eggs.

"In the dreams, there were… encounters… with these creatures…" She knew how what she was saying sounded.

"They were black, with thin, dark skin. Not unlike what I saw in the tree on Friday. They were tall—like over seven feet tall. The creatures were lean but clearly very strong. Their heads were slightly larger than a human head, and they had these large, black eyes, kind of like an owl's. And they didn't speak—there was nothing where their mouths should have been. Instead of talking, they… hummed…"

Nick had plated their breakfast and was now standing at the counter, looking intently at Kay, waiting for her to go on.

"The freakiest part is that they had this red, glowing, spiral arrow in the center of their chests. Like… exactly what Jonny described about the Umbravue. And just like what's on my shoulder." She didn't want to admit it. Nick didn't move.

"Hang on. Let me sketch it for you." She had to get the image out of her brain.

Kay got up, rummaged through a kitchen junk drawer, and pulled out an old legal pad and a ballpoint pen.

Back at the table, she started drawing. Nick still had not moved or said anything. Their breakfast sat on the counter, getting cold.

Finally, Nick woke up from his shock and joined her at the table. He placed a breakfast plate in front of each of them while he stared—unblinking—at Kay sketching.

"Here." Kay spun the drawing around in front of Nick.

Nick picked up the paper and studied it.

"Do you think this is what you saw while hunting on Friday? Up in the pine tree?" he asked after a minute or two.

"I'm not positive, because there were so many branches in the way, but that's how it looked," she answered.

"The most interesting part about seeing them in my dreams was that it felt like I *knew* them, and I was overcome with peace when I saw them in the dream. Like an incredible calm."

"Hmm." Nick was still studying the sketch.

"Can you pull up your left sleeve?" he asked.

Kay nodded. She knew what he was getting at, so she pulled up the heather gray sleeve of her Shadowflight Archery T-shirt.

"So, you saw these things in your dreams before you saw that on your shoulder this morning?" Nick asked, connecting the dots.

"Correct," Kay affirmed.

He looked at the drawing for another second. "That thing is scary as hell looking."

Nick grabbed the legal pad and flipped to a fresh page.

"Okay, let's outline all of this," he said with determination.

He started writing:

Friday — Went hunting in the morning. Saw bear or alien or cryptid or Umbravue? Came to Shadowflight in the afternoon. Then went to parents' house.

Saturday — went hunting in the morning. Lost over two hours of time. Fell from treestand. Metal carabiner melted into tree. Then witnessed a criminal. Helped neighbor. Started seeing into people's perspectives and feeling their emotions.

He stopped writing for a moment. "For the sake of organization, I'm going to call your power *ArrowVision*. Pretty cool name, right?"

He didn't wait for Kay to respond. He kept scribbling.

Came to Dee's cabin. Called me. Examined the area where you fell. Went to the casino to test ArrowVision. It seemed to work while playing poker. Overwhelmed by people's perspectives. Then went to Frankie's and Jonny claims the creatures are called the 'Umbravue.'
Sunday — Had dreams with—

Nick paused again. "Again, for organization, let's go with Jonny's name and call them the Umbravue?" he asked.

Kay shrugged. "Yeah, that's fine." Last night, Nick said Jonny was crazy, and now he was leaning into Jonny's story.

Nick kept writing.

—the Umbravue in them. Felt calm and peaceful when seeing them. Didn't feel like a dream. Woke up with spiral arrow brand on shoulder. Same spiral arrow symbol as on the Umbravue chests? Also, have felt good—like peaceful and calm—since getting ArrowVision.

He finished writing and held the legal pad at arm's length to review his work. "How does this all look to you?"

Nick placed the pad in front of Kay on the table. She studied it for a few minutes.

"I mean, yes. That is what has happened so far. Reading it makes it seem even stranger and more unreal," Kay confessed.

Do you know when you've stressed yourself out so much and been so overwhelmed by a situation that your brain finally gives in?

Example: You're incredibly nervous about getting a shot at the doctor's office, but after you wait in the waiting room and exam room for three hours, your nerves disappear, and you're just ready to get the shot over with and move on with your life.

Kay felt like that at that moment. She felt like she was so far down this rabbit hole, she would accept whatever was going on. She no longer felt anxious or panicky. Instead, she wanted answers.

Her phone buzzed.

Kay glanced down at her phone screen. It was a text from Pam McQuinn. "Can't wait to see you tomorrow at the Bicentennial! Be sure to dress nicely. Love you!"

Her mom always audited how Kay dressed in public, even at thirty years old. Appearances were everything.

When she looked up, Nick was staring at her, waiting for some input.

"Sorry, that was my mom," she said dismissively.

Then, with her phone in hand, she said, "Let me search 'Umbravue' real quick on the internet."

Kay typed into the search bar the word, and then different combinations of words—"Owlsbourne the Umbravue," "Native American the Umbravue," etc.

Nothing came up.

Jonny was right; maybe the Umbravue had been scrubbed from the internet. Or maybe Jonny made the whole thing up. Though that seemed less probable now.

She looked up from her phone. "Nothing. I say we go into town and test out ArrowVision more."

"I agree!" Nick exclaimed as he slapped both hands down on the glass table. Shotgun jumped at the loud bang. "Sorry, buddy," Nick apologized to the dog. "I didn't mean to ruin your nap…"

Kay was lost in thought. Nick could tell that she was distracted.

"Hey, do you want to talk about last night?" Nick asked as he placed his hand on Kay's.

"No," she answered, still not looking at him, her mind elsewhere. "I can confidently say that that has been the best part of this weekend."

She turned and smiled at him, then she shot out of her seat.

Kay was present now. Her mind was still distracted by everything that was happening, but she knew if she didn't get moving, she'd be stuck sitting here all day, drowning in the thick sludge of her own thoughts and questions.

"Let's do this," she suggested with an uncertain enthusiasm.

"All right then!" Nick answered as he picked up the legal pad and pen. "I'm taking these for notes."

They took Shotgun out once more and then locked up the cabin.

"I'll drive," Nick stated, without question.

Probably a good idea, Kay thought, since she didn't know how to control her visions.

Chapter 26

The next several hours were spent in the center of Owlsbourne. Nick noted that Kay seemed to get visions as soon as they were about 150 yards from the center of town—and from a lot of people.

Kay and Nick walked from store to store, waiting for visions.

What seemed true was that the calmer Kay remained, the better she could control what she saw in her mind.

Nick stood near her, and when she had a vision, she would tap his shoulder so he would be aware and take notes.

From Nick's perspective, Kay seemed calm and collected. There was nothing strange about her behavior, and when she had the visions, he couldn't even tell. All Nick saw was Kay blink. Just a normal blink—occasionally, the blink might be slightly longer than usual. They still hadn't figured out the timing between blinking and visions.

But for Kay, the world was an unbridled, wild stallion she was only meeting for the first time. Her life before this had been so dull. Having ArrowVision was like having sugar for the first time—overwhelming, sweet, and a bit addicting.

The catch? Kay was positive now that she only saw other people's perspectives when they were in a heightened state of stress. So, all the emotions she felt from other people while using ArrowVision were negative.

She didn't care, though. For the first time in years, she was living freely. She was uninhibited. Her brain felt free from the cell she'd locked it in. She wasn't obsessed or afraid or doubtful. She was just alive.

Kay didn't even care if she was crazy at this point. This weekend with Nick had been the best (albeit weirdest) weekend of her life.

Her brain buzzed as she and Nick wandered through the Owlsbourne shops. Nick scribbled fervently on the legal pad. Kay was discovering the secret lives and stresses of many people.

In most situations, she couldn't tell what their source of stress was. She could only see their current perspective and feel their emotions. She couldn't read their thoughts or *really* travel through time.

The power strictly existed in the moment.

When she slowed her breathing and cleared her mind, the visions would get slower, easier to understand, and more manageable. She clutched her wolf necklace for calm.

As she mastered the power, her proximity to each person became increasingly important. She would see the closest person's perspective first, but proximity didn't limit her visions. She could cycle through each person's perspective in her mind and choose the one she wanted to investigate further.

It was a lot like changing channels on a television.

As she stood among all the people, the visions became less of an overwhelming flurry and more like a calculated series of pictures in her head.

As she mastered ArrowVision, any panic subsided. ArrowVision felt more like an ultimate meditative state.

Nick turned to her. "You seem pretty calm," he observed.

"I really am," Kay confirmed.

"Then I say we move on to a bigger challenge. Let's go back to The Golden Sphinx," Nick suggested.

Kay hesitated.

"Not to play cards again. I think ArrowVision"—he said in a hushed tone—"would be tougher to control in such a stressful place."

Kay considered this for a moment. He had a point. Most of the people in town were just doing their Sunday shopping—not gambling their life's savings.

"Okay, let's do it," Kay agreed.

Nick tucked the legal pad under his arm and touched Kay's lower back, nudging her toward the Bronco.

"Well then, let's go, Super Woman."

As they walked out of the store, they heard over the loudspeaker: "Hi folks! Siren Hex speaking. You all know me as the Founder of BlackHole, but did you also know that Thanksgiving is my and my daughter's favorite—"

Chapter 27

12:23 p.m. – The Golden Sphinx was as dingy as ever. Somehow, it looked even worse than the day before.

Kay was bombarded with visions of different perspectives the moment the Bronco was about 150 yards away from the casino. The energy emanating from the casino was dark—not unlike the previous day. But now that the visions were less chaotic, Kay saw and felt the darkness more clearly.

They parked.

"This is going to be hard, Nick." Kay turned to him with genuine concern.

Nick turned to face her. He put a hand on each shoulder and looked her straight in the eyes. "I know that this is all unbelievably strange. But you are tough. Let's figure this out together. Tell me if you want to leave at any point, and we're out."

Before she could answer, his strong hand moved to the back of her head. He pulled her close and placed his soft, warm lips on hers.

Then he pulled away, winked, and hopped out of the truck—like nothing had happened. As if the world didn't completely stop every time they kissed.

Kay sat still, like a deer in the headlights.

Her phone buzzed. It was a text from her roommate, Carlo. "Hey, roomie! Just a heads up—the landlord stopped by for your half of the rent. She said you're 5 days late on payment. No worries! I sweet-talked her and bought you some time ;)"

"Come on! We don't have all day!" Nick shouted from outside the truck.

"Okay, okay!" Kay dragged herself out of the passenger side. She was already so overwhelmed by the emotions she was channeling from inside The Golden Sphinx.

"Before we go in there," Kay caught up with Nick and stopped him. "Why are you so invested in figuring this out with me?"

She had been wondering since yesterday. She certainly wanted a partner and the help, but she was puzzled about why Nick was so encouraging—and so cool—about everything.

Nick froze in precisely the spot where Kay had cried the day before. He looked her straight in the eyes.

"Superpowers, heroes, and myths give me hope that there is good in this world. That there is more than this," Nick answered earnestly, as he lifted his arms and gestured to The Golden Sphinx and its sad surroundings.

"I don't know if you have a power, Kay, but if you do, it gives me hope. And if you don't, well… I've had a crush on you for a long time, and it is fun hanging out. Even if we're *both* crazy, that won't stop me from finally taking my shot with you."

Kay studied his face.

Then Nick admitted, "If ArrowVision is real, that would be amazing! Heck, I want to be able to use ArrowVision— how wild! I think everyone wants to be special… I guess. So, if I can help you with this, even a little, it makes me feel like I'm doing something… good. That sounds stupid."

Kay took his hand. He answered so honestly.

"ArrowVision is just taking the time to understand other people's perspectives. In a way, anyone could do it."

He looked at her as if he had never thought of that. "I guess you're right."

They said nothing more. Instead, they turned and walked hand in hand toward The Golden Sphinx.

Nick was right—being at The Golden Sphinx was much more challenging. Kay's stomach turned the second they walked through the entrance. She wanted to run to the bathroom again. Her brain was unbearably overstimulated.

She squeezed her eyes shut and stood, paralyzed, in the center of The Golden Sphinx's foyer.

The whirring and dinging of the machines assaulted Kay's ears. In the distance, over the loudspeaker, she heard again:

"Hi folks! Siren Hex speaking. You all know me as the Founder of BlackHole, but did you also know that Thanksgiving is my and my daughter's favorite holiday? What better way to show our appreciation for Owlsbourne—"

Nick noticed Kay's discomfort. He leaned over to whisper in her ear, "Just breathe. You've got this. Take your time."

Kay took a breath… and another.

Her thoughts started to organize themselves. She opened her eyes.

Nick guided her to a seat at a bar.

"No alcohol," Nick insisted. "We can't mess with the results in any way."

"Okay…" She agreed hesitantly.

Kay could really go for a gin and tonic right now.

They ordered two Cokes and some french fries so as not to draw attention to the fact that they were camped out at a bar, staring at every passerby. Kay placed her Coke on an

Allerzil-branded cocktail napkin. Her art was always there, haunting her.

The emotions Kay felt while using ArrowVision were staggering. With each mental vision, she actually *felt*, in her soul, a range of deeply negative emotions. That was certainly the downside to ArrowVision.

Kay thought for a moment about all the people in town earlier—about Maya, about the criminal in the car, about all these sad people at the casino. It was at this moment that Kay realized most everyone had a difficult time existing, not just her. People who seemed so put-together on the outside struggled so much on the inside.

Kay had never really taken the time to feel the pain in others because she had been ignorantly—or selfishly— blinded by her own problems.

All these people she was using ArrowVision on were just trying to survive, the best way they knew how.

As she and Nick sat at the bar, Kay cycled through visions in her mind and reported what she saw, in a hushed tone, to Nick, who scribbled down notes.

At first, Kay could not control which perspectives she saw. She simply saw the perspective of whoever was closest to her.

However, as time passed, she fine-tuned ArrowVision. When she blinked, she would cycle through the perspectives in her mind until she found the one she wanted to see more of—again, a lot like changing channels on a television.

As she viewed people's different perspectives, she saw clammy hands, twitching legs, sweaty brows, and overall physical tension in almost every scene.

She saw nothing exceptional—just the occasional *you owe me money* text or empty bank account receipt.

After about an hour of observation, she and Nick decided to call it quits and head back to Dee's cabin to discuss their findings.

Chapter 28

Back in the parking lot, leaving The Golden Sphinx, Kay was overcome with her most vivid vision yet.

In her mind, she saw the interior of what seemed to be an old truck. The dash and steering wheel looked like they were transported from another era. The long bench seat was made of gray, soft fabric, and the steering wheel had a Ford emblem in the center. At first glance and smell, the truck was well-maintained and clean.

The incredible stress of the person inside the truck suffocated Kay.

As she observed the scene through their eyes, she realized it was a man's perspective. Not just any man—it was Jimmy, the owner of Shadowflight Archery.

Kay recognized his black Shadowflight Archery work shirt right away. His Shadowflight employee name tag— Jimmy—sat turned up in the cupholder.

Jimmy was sitting on the driver's side of the truck. In the vision, he looked down at paperwork strewn across the bench. Tears welled in his eyes.

Kay couldn't control Jimmy's actions, nor could she see everything in the truck—only what he looked at. However, as he stared at the paperwork, she read the headers. One piece of paper on a stack said *State of Connecticut Superior Court* in the center and *Summons – Civil* on the top left. The document appeared to be a court summons for an unpaid credit card debt of $11,435.

She felt sweat bead down the side of Jimmy's temple, and then a tear dripped onto his perfectly pressed Shadowflight shirt. The back of his calloused right hand wiped the tears from his cheek.

Kay could feel the stress and anguish all the way in the pit of Jimmy's stomach.

Besides the court summons papers, there was another— maybe more detrimental—document. This one read *Divorce Agreement* at the top, with Jimmy's signature scrawled at the bottom.

As far as Kay knew, Jimmy was happily married with three beautiful children. Jimmy and his family were a staple in Owlsbourne—a true example of the dream American family.

Kay felt Jimmy clutch something cold and plastic in his left hand. The pills rattled against the bottle as his hand shook with nervousness.

Jimmy turned his head to stare at the orange pharmacy bottle. Kay noticed the label. It was a prescription for powerful painkillers. Jimmy opened the bottle as sweat poured down his face. Then he dumped all the pills into his right hand.

He was going to overdose.

Kay snapped back to reality. Nick was riveted, looking at her when she opened her eyes.

Distressed and frantic, Kay yelled at Nick, "What kind of car does Jimmy drive?!"

Nick was stunned and confused. "My boss, Jimmy?"

"YES!" Kay was screaming now. She had taken off walking briskly through The Golden Sphinx parking lot.

"Ummm…" Nick thought out loud while chasing Kay. "It's a red '90s F-150," Nick shouted ahead to her.

Kay urgently weaved through the maze of vehicles in the enormous Golden Sphinx parking lot. She was running now.

"What the hell?" she screamed back at Nick, who was still a few feet behind. "He has to be here!"

"Who? Jimmy?" Nick asked, out of breath.

Kay didn't answer. She stopped for a moment and scanned the parking lot with her eyes. Nothing. Where was the truck?

As she turned to speak to Nick, she noticed a red, old truck diagonally across from her in the adjoining QuikCash parking lot.

Kay took off sprinting toward the F-150. The November sun beat down, offset by a cool fall breeze. The truck seemed so far away, but it was probably only about one hundred yards from where she was standing when she saw it.

The asphalt slammed against the bottom of Kay's combat boots. She heard Nick's footsteps trailing her.

Kay's momentum caused her to slam into the candy-apple red hood of the truck. With both hands spread on the hood to brace herself, she looked up.

Kay didn't see Jimmy's perspective. She was learning to control ArrowVision. The more focused she was, the less intrusive the visions were.

Instead, through the windshield, through her own eyes, she saw her friend slumped on the driver's side of the vehicle, crying. His cheeks were wet and glistening in the sunlight. Jimmy did not look up. He was still conscious.

Kay ran to the driver's side and pounded on the window. Nick was with her now. He joined in the pounding.

After about thirty seconds, Jimmy slowly gazed up at them. His eyes were droopy and distant. The pain pills were doing their job.

Nick slammed on the window. "Open the door, Jimmy!"

Jimmy just stared and shook his head—no—as tears streamed from his cloudy eyes.

Kay called 911 on her cell while Nick ran to the passenger's side. He tore off his button-up shirt, wrapped it around his fist and forearm. Nick took a step back. "Kay, stay over there," he insisted.

A minute later, Nick's fist punched through the window.

As Nick and Kay pulled Jimmy out of the truck and laid him on his side, Kay got a brief, hazy, sleepy glimpse of Jimmy's perspective through ArrowVision.

It was the purest sadness Kay had ever felt.

The ambulance arrived moments later. The paramedics laid Jimmy on the gurney and began trying to rid his body of the toxic pills.

Chapter 29

Once the scene settled, the lead paramedic approached Kay and Nick, who were sitting outside the QuikCash on a broken, old metal bench. Kay was busy picking the chipping blue paint off the bench when the thirty-something-year-old paramedic approached her.

"Hey, how is he doing?" Kay jumped up and asked the paramedic while he was still a few feet away. Nick followed.

"He's doing well. He'll be just fine. Thank goodness you all noticed him in the truck. We honestly got here just in time. Had we been here a few minutes later, we would be having a very different conversation. Good work." He placed his hands on both their shoulders, gave them a nod, and then walked back toward the ambulance.

Kay turned to Nick. "Shit." She was mentally and physically exhausted. She had been fighting off ArrowVision episodes all afternoon. Even though she was getting better at filtering them, she was not a pro yet.

Nick could tell she was spent. He said nothing. Instead, he embraced her in the safest hug she had ever felt—and he didn't let go.

Then he whispered in her ear, half-jokingly, "Man, I guess ArrowVision works. Does that mean you're a hero?" Then he lowered his voice to an intentionally creepy tone. "Or an alien?"

Kay, breaking through her despair and exhaustion, let out a quiet laugh.

She pulled away. They were both sort of smiling, desperate for that slight bit of comedic relief.

"Let's go," Nick suggested, gesturing toward the Bronco. "Dinner is on me," he insisted.

"Okay. I'll take you up on that," Kay agreed, as she slowly, solemnly started walking away from the QuikCash.

As soon as Kay stepped off the curb and into the QuikCash parking lot, another vision struck—a vision more overpowering than anything she'd felt before. Even the one with Jimmy hadn't hit this hard.

Chapter 30

In her mind, Kay was inside the QuikCash—in a dark back room or a basement.

Kay only knew it was the QuikCash because she saw the QuikCash logo on a wall.

Whoever's perspective she was in was… different. It was glitchy, like channels on a television; this channel had static. It was like trying to watch a television with an antenna instead of cable.

She seemed to be seeing a man's perspective. He was sitting in an uncomfortable metal chair, nervously bouncing his left leg. His blue jeans were torn and dirty. From what Kay could see, he wore a raggedy white T-shirt that hung on his skinny frame.

Then the vision glitched out.

She suddenly lost the entire scene and was back in the parking lot with Nick.

Except this time, when she came to, she was staggering.

Nick quickly grabbed her arm and helped steady her while he waited for Kay to regain her balance.

"Whoa, what the hell just happened?" Nick asked, concerned. "You clearly had a vision. But unlike all your other visions, you looked like you were in a trance. Almost like you were in pain."

"I saw inside the QuikCash, but this time I couldn't see clearly—like something was jamming the signal," Kay answered, still in a daze. She sat back down on the blue bench.

"Okay, we should go, Kay. I don't like this. Maybe we've pushed things too far."

"Just give me a minute," Kay said, raising her hand to silence Nick. "I just need to think. That was really weird."

Now, she did feel like a superhero—or an alien. Nick sat down beside her and gave her space to gather her thoughts.

"I'm going to try to control ArrowVision and jump back into that perspective. The guy seemed agitated and anxious."

"Doesn't every vision you jump into feel like that?" Nick was genuinely curious.

"Yes… but this was… different. Something was off about the whole thing." She pushed, "I want to see what's going on."

"Okay, well, I'm right here with you." He grabbed and held her hand as tightly as he could.

"Thank you." Kay was in the zone. Then, she closed her eyes and jumped back into the visions. She cycled through the vision channels in her mind until she found the QuikCash scene.

Chapter 31

The scene was still glitchy. This time, she could feel the sweat pouring down the man's forehead and pooling, warm, on the back of his neck.

He had something in his hand. Kay noticed there were two other people in the room. One was standing near the man. She couldn't make out the person's face. Again, the vision had a lot of static.

She could discern that the room was small, like a storage closet. The air was thick and suffocating, carrying the musty scent of neglect. A dim lightbulb flickered overhead. The walls were peeling. On the other side of the room was an old, wooden desk. The third person was sitting at the desk, taking notes.

The man glanced down at his hand, and Kay could see what he was holding. It was a small pill that glowed a metallic orange. Kay had never seen anything like it.

Then, as the man shifted in the creaky metal chair, the standing figure in the room approached him.

"Here's your money; don't spend it all in one place," the figure scoffed, in a low, cigarette-burned growl, and handed the man a stack of cash.

Kay could feel the coarse bills beneath the man's fingertips. The man shoved the wad of cash into his front pocket.

She could feel his nervousness. The man's heart raced. His muscles were tense, constricted into fight-or-flight mode.

The figure at the desk looked up at him from across the room. Kay still couldn't see the figure's face. It was a blurry, static vision that Kay was fighting to stay in. The figure seemed to have the shape of a woman.

"Go ahead and take your dose. We want to see you back here in a week. Of course, we will have your next payment ready for you then," the woman instructed.

Kay would recognize that voice anywhere.

It was the voice of Siren Hex.

What the hell was Siren Hex, a famous billionaire and the CEO of BlackHole, doing in the back of the seedy QuikCash?

The man raised his shaking hand to his mouth and swallowed the metallic orange pill.

Then Kay lost the vision again. She was back on the bench with Nick.

"What happened? What did you see? You were really… absorbed… You looked like you were hypnotized," Nick explained, still holding her hand.

Now, Kay's heart was racing, and she felt lightheaded. The world spun around her. She squeezed her eyes shut and started talking to distract herself.

"I don't know…" she began. "The vision I was in—I think the man was terrified. But I couldn't see things clearly, like it was a static, glitchy channel. I couldn't fully discern details or faces. It wasn't at all like any of my other visions."

The pounding of her heart was deafening. Could Nick hear the loud thudding emanating from her chest?

He rubbed her back. "Okay, take a breath. Focus," he said soothingly.

Kay breathed. "Something was wrong about the whole situation, and I think… No, I know… Siren Hex was there."

"*The* Siren Hex? Why in the world would she ever be in a dump like that?" he asked, pointing to the QuikCash.

"I don't know, Nick. I think that's what we need to find out."

Chapter 32

The ride back to Dee's cabin felt infinite. Kay was overwhelmed. The inside of the Bronco was burning up. She had to get out. She felt like a trapped animal.

Kay couldn't ground herself. The outside scenery blurred through the car windows—too fast for her to process. Her mind spiraled, and her chest felt heavy. Upside down felt right side up. The sky looked immense and crushing. A familiar monster of panic rose from the depths of Kay's subconscious, clawing at her brain as it let out a hideous howl.

Despite ArrowVision making her feel calm a lot of the time, Kay couldn't avoid her own deep emotions.

"Pull over!" she spat out at Nick. "Pull over now!"

Kay dove out of the car, bent over the cold metal guardrail, and threw up.

She sat on the ground and stared up at the sky. The leaves crunched under the weight of her thoughts. Kay knew she looked crazy sitting on the side of the road, but she needed to feel the earth with her hands for a moment and get her head straight. She closed her eyes and breathed.

Then, she felt a kind hand touch her shoulder.

"Hey, it's okay," Nick whispered. He was sitting next to her in the dirt as cars whizzed by.

Tears rolled down her cheeks. "It's not okay," Kay answered meekly.

She was soaked in embarrassment. Why couldn't she be more put-together—less emotional, less affected by everything?

"I don't know what I'm doing. Am I in some weird, warped reality? This all feels insane. And Siren Hex? She's one of the most powerful businesspeople not only in Owlsbourne but in the world," Kay trailed off as she stared at a squirrel in the trees beyond the guardrail.

She squeezed her wolf necklace. *A joke from Penny about this whole bizarre situation would be perfect right about now.*

As she started to feel grounded, her thoughts began to organize themselves. The panic attack was passing, leaving Kay clearer-headed than ever.

"Who cares who Siren is? If she is doing something bad, we should find out," Nick stated without hesitation.

Kay took a moment. She crumpled the dry fallen leaves under her fingertips, reminding herself that she was still, in fact, on this planet.

"You're right," she agreed.

Chapter 33

3:37 p.m. – Back at Dee's cabin, Shotgun, Kay, and Nick sat on the living room floor in a powwow with Kay's laptop and a fresh Frankie's pepperoni pizza in the center of the circle.

"Why would Siren Hex be at the creepy QuikCash?" Kay wondered aloud.

"And you said that there was an orange, metallic pill she was encouraging someone to take?" Nick asked, as Shotgun gnawed on a pig ear in the corner of the room.

"Yes, exactly," Kay answered as she started clacking on her laptop keys, searching for anything and everything about Siren Hex, BlackHole, pills—anything that seemed relevant.

"Okay," Nick noted. He took the hint and started investigating BlackHole on his phone.

For the next hour, Kay and Nick scoured the internet for any clues about Siren Hex and BlackHole. They came up with nothing.

Strangely, there weren't many articles about BlackHole or Siren Hex at all. For a multi-billion-dollar company and a world-renowned CEO, all the searchable information was squeaky clean. There were only positive press releases and interviews. It was almost as if any negativity related to BlackHole had been wiped from the internet.

"Wait… I think I got something," Nick said, getting up and moving over next to Kay on the floor while staring at his phone.

"Check out this comment on this Zeddit feed."

The title of the Zeddit thread read: Corporate Cover-Ups. Nick had scrolled down to the absolute last, most buried comment. Kay read it aloud:

MrStrange_8937: u guys should check out blak whole.

"Whoa, good find. But is that all that's on the internet? Some weird, misspelled message board comment?" Kay was frustrated.

Kay and Nick looked at each other for a moment, totally disappointed.

"Okay, well, let's at least send a message to MrStrange_8937," Kay suggested as she logged into her Zeddit account on Nick's phone, ready to craft a message. Nick scooted up next to her, both leaning against the couch.

Nick gently touched her leg for reassurance as his shoulder rested against hers.

Kay turned toward him, and before his full face came into view, he kissed her—soft and sweet. Then he pulled back.

"Let's go, girl! We've got a mystery to solve," Nick joked, pointing at the phone in her hands.

"Okay, okay," Kay relented.

She started typing from her Zeddit account, username: KMQArcher23.

KMQArcher23: *Hey! I saw your comment about BlackHole. Do you know anything about cover-ups or corruption there?*

"I don't know. Does that look good?" Kay asked.

"Sure. Send it," Nick gestured.

Kay hit send. Before she could put the phone down to continue researching, a notification popped up. Kay and Nick read the screen together:

MrStrange_8937: *email me at MrStrange_8937@secrtspi.com. do not write blak whole.*

"This feels weird…"

"It's probably some guy in his mom's basement, and this will lead nowhere. We might as well email him, and then we don't have to engage anymore if we don't want to," Nick said calmly.

"Okay."

Kay started typing from her email address:

Hi. I messaged you on Zeddit for information about blak whole cover-ups and corruption.

Sent.

Again, her computer instantly dinged with a reply.

Security on break at 12:45 a.m. for 10 mins. No one manning cameras then. I'll glitch security system for exactly 10 minutes. Enter south side entrance. Park far away. Corner office. Office – first door on left. Entry code SH 56834. Key under owl. File name "SEE"

Kay and Nick turned to each other, bewildered. Shotgun snored in the corner as the cheese of the uneaten pizza began to cool and harden.

"What the… This is too sketchy," Kay said in disbelief.

"I agree," Nick answered as he turned the laptop toward himself and read the message again. "Let's respond and see if they're legit. Like, if they'll meet us."

"Okay," Kay answered. They were already this far into it—what was one more email?

Thank you for your response. Are you able to meet or do a video call?

Kay's computer pinged with a reply. This time, the message wasn't from the sender—it was from the web host.

Error: We won't be able to deliver this message to MrStrange_8937@secrtspi.com because the email address is no longer valid.

"What the hell? This officially got so much weirder," Nick admitted, concern washing over his face.

Kay leaned back, her spine pressed uncomfortably against the square, modern sofa. She stayed silent and thought for a moment.

"SH…" Kay said, thinking out loud.

Nick shrugged. "Honestly, it's probably just some lunatic conspiracy theorist on the internet. Maybe we shouldn't have messaged them."

"What could SH stand for?" Kay sat in the stillness, racking her brain for an answer.

She paused. "Siren Hex!" she blurted out. "Obviously!" Kay was disappointed with herself for not seeing what was right in front of her.

"And that must be the code to her office!" Kay was familiar with the BlackHole security systems from visiting her dad at work. All entryways required a keycard to enter, and then the C-level employees—and higher—had auto-locking doors for their offices. Each office door had its own keypad and entry code. Kay explained the security system to Nick.

"So, you think this stranger on an internet chatroom just told us the code to the office of one of the most successful businesspeople in the world?" Nick asked in disbelief.

Kay felt embarrassed that she was getting sucked down this rabbit hole. She already thought this surreal weekend couldn't be real. Now this?

Then Nick threw his hands up in a "whatever" gesture and said, "Fuck it. That would not be the weirdest thing that happened this weekend."

A huge smile stretched across his face as he started lightheartedly laughing—maybe out of discomfort, maybe out of excitement, or maybe because he, like Kay, finally felt full-tilt crazy.

Kay let out a soft, hesitant laugh as she started typing in the search bar on her laptop. She made eye contact with Nick. "Let's get into this office, then."

For the next several hours, in Dee's cozy wood cabin, Nick and Kay strategized their BlackHole break-in plan. All the while, Shotgun slept on the rug, occasionally yelping as he chased after an elusive squirrel in his dreams.

Chapter 34

11:17 p.m. – Kay could hear Nick's soft breath, in and out, as he slept beside her. The bedside alarm clock read *11:17 p.m.* The chic taupe linen sheets that the realtor had staged the bed with gently embraced Kay's bare skin, soaking in any lingering beads of sweat. Her shoulder still throbbed with pain where the spiral welt had now deflated into a pink, spiral scar.

What is happening? she thought to herself as she stared blankly at the ceiling. Light from the full moon pierced through the bedroom window, as if it were a spotlight, highlighting her strange existence.

She couldn't sleep. How could she? There were too many thoughts swirling around in her head. Plus, she feared that if she fell asleep, she might reencounter the Umbravue.

Instead, she mentally mapped out their BlackHole break-in plan. She would "borrow" her dad's BlackHole keycard from his car during the Owlsbourne Bicentennial Celebration. Then, she and Nick would sneak into the BlackHole headquarters and follow the clues from the online tipster.

Kay's eyes traced the long shadows around the bedroom. The bedside clock ticked like an eerie metronome, in time with her heartbeat. Suddenly, the moon's silver glow that illuminated the room faded into darkness, as if something was blocking the window.

Kay had the unsettling feeling that she was being watched.

She slowly rolled her body to face the first-story window. She noticed that the crickets chirping outside had gone silent—and that Shotgun's soothing, quiet snoring had ceased. As she rolled, her eyes peeked just over Nick's shoulder to see a black figure standing inches from the house, outside the window.

The figure was so tall that part of its head was cut off by the window frame. It was thin and lanky. Kay again noticed that it had nothing where its mouth should have been. The creature's two enormous, glassy eyes—black and reflective—consumed most of its face and were devoid of whites. They were endless pools of darkness that peered into the deadly quiet bedroom. In the moonlight, Kay could see a dimpling of the creature's skin, resembling a plucked chicken; the black skin seemed to have bumps where feathers used to be.

The most distinguishable feature was the glowing, red, arrow spiral on the creature's chest.

The silhouette outside was still.

Then, a subtle, low humming sound started to reverberate through the house.

Kay wanted to wake Nick. She wanted to scream; she wanted to run—but her body lay frozen, immobile. Her eyes were fixated on the dark being. Her instincts told her not to move at all.

The creature leaned closer and observed, with a disturbing intensity, as if it could see not only through the window but into the depths of Kay's mind.

Though visually terrifying, its presence was calm and peaceful. It seemed to have an ancient intelligence. The creature's head tilted almost ninety degrees, like an owl, as if trying to decide what to do next. Then it raised one of its sharp, talon-like fingers and gently tapped the glass—*tap, tap, tap.* Then it curled the finger back in a "come here" gesture, as if to say to Kay, *Come outside with me.*

The dull humming sound transformed into a piercing screech, like some sort of beacon. In response, the creature rotated its head almost 360 degrees—again like an owl— looking into the woods, as if it had accomplices waiting in the trees somewhere. Then it turned back, looked at Kay one last time, and scurried out of view.

Stunned, Kay glanced over to Shotgun, who had been sleeping on a makeshift bed of blankets on the floor in the opposite corner of the room. Shotgun's expressive hound eyes were wide and terrified, fixated on the window.

That was it. Kay needed to know what was going on. Her fear was eclipsed by absolute frustration. *What was going on with her? With her body? What did these things want?* Was she even living in reality anymore? She still secretly hoped it was the Bennett boys or their kids playing a prank on her.

Overcome with emotion and the need for answers, Kay leaped out of bed. She tossed on a T-shirt, pajama pants, and her beat-up combat boots, grabbed her Ruger .22 from the closet, and ran out of the room toward the front door.

Kay wasn't thinking. She was only driven by adrenaline and a need for explanations. *How dare anyone mess with Dee's house and property—even if they were aliens!*

Outside, her breath came in sharp gasps as she scanned the yard, left to right. She stood about twenty yards from the front door of the cabin under the bright, white light of the floodlight. Her ears strained to identify any strange, unfamiliar sounds. She didn't see any creatures or people. The humming had stopped.

Kay shouted into the nothingness, "Come out here! Mikey Bennett, I swear if that's you, I'm going to shoot your ass!"

Mikey was Merle Bennett's oldest son and the worst of the bunch.

Kay's eyes adjusted to the blackness of the woods. That's when she saw it: glowing red spiral arrows etched into the trunk of each tree within eyesight. The red symbols didn't flicker like fire but instead seemed to breathe—pulsing, as if each tree had its own heartbeat.

The forest's crimson glow intensified as Kay took one shaky step forward.

The humming sound began again, in rhythm with the pulsing, red, spiral arrows. The woods were chanting. The chant felt primal and prehistoric. The trees, the animals, and the earth were conjuring something. Kay was looking at a living, breathing forest that pulsed with a life of its own.

She felt peace.

Kay had been so entranced that she hadn't noticed that both Shotgun and Nick had followed her out of the cabin.

Nick's voice was distant, though he was only a few yards behind her. *What was he saying?* Kay couldn't focus; her mind was consumed by the woods and the hum. *hmmmmmmmmmmm*

"KAY!"

She could hear Nick better now, but his words were still far away.

"KAY!"

"KAY! WHAT IS GOING ON?!"

"KAY, LOOK AT ME!"

That last plea was clear in Kay's ears.

She pulled her eyes away from the woods and turned to face Nick.

"Kay! What the…?"

Before she could say anything, she followed Nick's gaze down to her own two feet.

It was then that she realized her feet—and her body—were levitating about a foot above the ground.

Chapter 35

Kay hung in the air, suspended like a marionette, right there in front of Dee's cabin.

She looked back up at Nick, who was speechless. His navy blue and black checkered boxer briefs hung on his hips. His dark hair was messy and pressed to one side from lying on the pillow. Nick's sleepy eyes were wide with amazement and horror. He stared at Kay's feet.

Then the tension broke. Kay fell to the ground with a hard thud.

The woods went black and quiet—no hum, no red spiral lights, not even the rustle of a leaf, the chirp of a cricket, or the distant hoot of an owl: dead silence and pure darkness.

Shotgun ran over to Kay, licking her face, ensuring that she was okay. Nick followed.

Kay hit the ground with so much force, she should have gotten a jolt of pain—but she didn't. She felt good, despite the lack of sleep, the crazy circumstances, and falling from midair to the ground.

"What the fuck, what the fuck, what the fuck," Kay repeated as she tried to sit up.

"HOLY SHIT! YOU WERE FLYING!" Nick shouted, even though Kay's face was now only a few feet from his own.

"What was that!? The trees were glowing red, and you looked like you were in a trance! Total deer in the headlights!" he continued.

Adrenaline coursed through Kay's veins. She felt so alive, so clear-headed.

Nick knelt down and grabbed Kay's hand to help pull her into a sitting position.

"Did you see the creature in the window?" Kay asked pointedly.

"Creature?" Nick shook his head. "No, by the time I got out here, all I saw was you, like… levitating… and the trees were all lit up. No creatures. Actually, no life at all. Not even a moth. Everything was silent aside from that low humming sound."

"Nick, the Umbravue are real. I saw one, and I followed it out here."

Kay was willing to dismiss this whole weekend as a fever dream or some weird form of going crazy, but now she believed it all.

"I—" she stammered, her voice trembling. "I thought this was all in my head. I thought I was going crazy."

Nick moved closer.

Then, out of nowhere, like it was implanted in her brain, Kay had the thought: *You are not crazy. You are chosen.*

She closed her eyes. Tears slipped down her cheeks. Her whole life, Kay had longed for a sense of purpose. And now, as the weight of the impossible pressed down on her, she felt both exhilarated and terrified. Her mind was racing. She had resisted all of this—brushing aside the strange spiral symbol, the visions in her head, the way she'd felt since falling out of the tree: calm, confident, healed—and the creatures that seemed to be following her.

Nick said nothing. He wrapped his arms around her as Shotgun sat protectively next to Kay.

After a minute or two, Kay finally opened her eyes. They were bloodshot from sleep deprivation and crying earlier.

She looked up at Nick.

"What do we do now?" she asked.

Chapter 36

11:41 p.m. – Kay, Nick, and Shotgun sat on the bed in the cabin. The bedroom was lit by a faint flicker from the dying fire in the woodstove in the other room.

Kay stood up, her arms tightly wrapped around herself as she paced back and forth. Nick sat on the edge of the bed, staring at her. He said nothing. He was in shock.

There was a long silence—just the crackling echo of embers and the sound of their breaths.

Then Nick said, "You levitated."

Kay nodded, slowly.

"I watched your feet leave the ground."

Nick recalled a bad dream. "I ran outside, and you were, like... hypnotized by the trees... which were glowing with the spiral arrow symbol, by the way... then your body just started lifting off the ground."

Kay flinched.

"I didn't ask for any of this."

"Ask for it? Who cares... You flew, Kay! It's... unbelievable... It's amazing."

Kay looked down at her hands, then at her feet.

"Did it feel… weird?" Nick asked.

"No. It felt easy…"

Kay was visibly distraught. She thought for a moment, then added, "Didn't Jonny say something about them flying? And I swear, when I saw the Umbravue in the tree on Friday, it looked like it floated for a moment. Maybe because they're associated with owls... They can fly…"

Kay knew how stupid this sounded—but she had just done it. She had just defied gravity.

"I just want to be normal again." Her head hung as she squeezed her wolf necklace.

"Kay, this doesn't change who you are," Nick asserted. He was up from the bed now, holding both of her hands.

"Doesn't it?" Kay asked.

Nick looked into Kay's eyes. "Whatever this all is… we'll figure it out."

Because they had no explanations, they had to accept the levitating as another part of the extraordinarily bizarre puzzle. Their eyelids were screaming with exhaustion.

Nick made sure the doors and windows were locked as Kay climbed back into bed—this time with the .22 and Shotgun by her side.

Nick spread a blanket over her and crawled into the bed beside her. The weight of everything unsaid pressed down on them, but they were just too tired. Kay's breathing slowed, and her fingers curled around Nick's, even while they slept.

Tomorrow, they would have to face the impossible again. But for now, under the light of the moon, they had a moment of quiet.

Chapter 37

MONDAY

6:23 a.m. – *Did I fly last night?* was Kay's first thought as she opened her eyes. She blinked sleepily and rolled over to stare at the window that had caused so much chaos the night before.

Nick felt Kay move next to him. "Is it morning already?" he mumbled, his voice rough from sleep.

His strong arm wrapped tightly around Kay as he pulled her closer and buried his face in her hair.

"Afraid so," Kay replied, her tone soft and distant.

After a minute or two, Nick snapped to attention, as if he had just joined the real world. "Oh my gosh—you *flew* last night!"

Kay didn't move; she kept her eyes trained on the window, secretly hoping that the Umbravue would reappear.
"I know," was all she said.

"We have to figure this stuff out, Nick. I'm all in—crazy or not," she continued.

Without even a moment of hesitation, Nick answered, "Hell yeah, let's do this." He kissed the back of her head and jumped out of bed.

He was so oddly optimistic all the time.

Shotgun remained at the foot of the bed. The drama of the night before had worn him out. He rolled onto his back, paws in the air, groaning as if the effort of existing before noon was too much to bear.

Nick came over to Kay's side of the bed, where she was still lying and staring distantly.

A sleepy smile spread across Kay's face as Nick knelt down to face her at the edge of the bed.

His dark eyes were soft, crinkling at the edges as he returned her gaze. He brushed a strand of hair from her face, tucking it behind her ear.

"You're staring," she said, embarrassed, covering her face with her hands.

Nick took both of her hands and gently removed them.

"Can't help it," Nick replied, his voice warm and steady.

He leaned in, his hand sliding to hold her jaw. Their lips met. Her arms unfolded, reaching out to pull him closer. His other hand slipped under the hem of her T-shirt.

The kiss deepened.

When they finally broke apart, her cheeks were flushed, and his grin had turned slightly mischievous.

"We're going to be late for work. We have to go about our normal day, so no one suspects anything is going on," she said, trying to sound stern.

"Shower then?" he suggested, his tone light but his eyes still holding that same intensity.

She laughed, already getting up and walking toward the bathroom.

Chapter 38

It wasn't that Kay and Nick were okay with what was happening; they were just so shell-shocked by it all. They knew that the only way out was through.

Over the next hour, they got dressed and packed their things to leave the cabin. Kay knew the realtor was showing the cabin to a potential buyer at 10:00 a.m. She had been tracking the sale of the house through the real estate app the realtor had recommended.

Kay and Nick would reconvene tonight at the Bicentennial Celebration. Until then, they decided to go about their regular workdays.

Nick would go to his shift at Shadowflight, and Kay would pretend everything was fine while watching the time drip by at Mytherra.

8:20 a.m. – Gravel crunched under their boots as they stepped onto the driveway to pack their trucks.

They both glanced back at the cabin and the property. The soft light of dawn cast a golden sheen over the woods. It was all so beautiful.

Before they went to their cars, they checked the trees for any spiral markings from the night before, but they found nothing—again.

"We're going to figure this out, right?" Kay asked Nick, keeping her eyes locked on the cabin.

"Right. Now, get your cute butt to work. And if you have any issues with ArrowVision throughout the day, call me— I will have my phone on loud," Nick said the last part very seriously.

"Okay," Kay agreed, her eyes widened as she remembered something. "Shoot, I forgot my phone in the cabin. You go ahead."

"Are you sure you'll be okay? I can wait until you leave," Nick said, worried about her safety.

"Yeah, I'll be fine. Go to work, you're going to be late," Kay pushed, as she looked at the time on her watch.

"Okay, okay." Nick kissed her, then jumped into the driver's seat of the Bronco.

He revved the engine and gave Kay a wink as he backed down the driveway.

Kay stood in the front yard with Shotgun, breathing in the forest air.

She forgot her phone, but she also wanted to have a moment alone with Dee's property. Despite everything that had happened over the last few days, this was still where she felt safest and happiest.

She closed her eyes and listened to the squirrels running through the leaves, the mourning doves singing, and the distant tapping of a woodpecker.

Then, she walked inside, grabbed her phone, and locked up.

Kay tossed her backpack into the backseat of her Jeep and opened the passenger door for Shotgun to hop into the front.

As she turned the key, the car radio came to life, playing the same annoying BlackHole ad:
"—before they're all gone! From all of us here at BlackHole, thank you! Remember, we're wiring minds for tomorrow!"

Out of habit, Kay checked her rearview mirror before backing up.

That was when she saw it.

There, in the mirror, was a creature—*the* creature.

Between two leafless trees, against the backdrop of the gray-blue cloudy sky, a black silhouette hung suspended in the air.

The creature was about forty feet above the ground and probably seventy yards behind Kay's Jeep.

Its arms were spread wide, and its long talon fingers were splayed open against the clouds. Its legs were pressed together in a "T" formation. The long talons on its feet pointed downward. Kay couldn't see any details because the silhouette was so black. All she could make out was the glowing red spiral arrow on its chest.

A chill darted up her spine.

She spun around in the driver's seat to peer out the back window, but the creature was gone when she looked up at the sky.

Chapter 39

Kay, driving with one hand on the wheel, fumbled for her phone. Shotgun lay calmly in the passenger seat as Kay swerved down the road. She had to call Nick.

"Come on, come on—pick up!" she said aloud to no one.

"Miss me already?" Nick answered playfully.

"I just saw one in the sky. I'm not kidding. It was floating between the tops of the trees. It had giant talons and a glowing red spiral arrow in the center of its chest, and then it just… disappeared."

Kay was frantic. Shotgun whined next to her. She rubbed his head and parked in the middle of a back road.

"Wait, what? Are you okay?" Nick's playful tone was gone.

"I'm fine. I swear I'm not making this up. It was huge and black—so black." She exhaled hard, eyes darting up to the empty sky.

Kay got her thoughts together and revved back up the engine while still on the phone with Nick. She remembered she had to get Shotgun back to her apartment in time before she got to work.

"Okay, okay, breathe. We'll figure this out. Just get to work safely, alright?" Nick was in protective mode.

Even though Nick couldn't see her, Kay nodded, her free hand white-knuckling the wheel.

"I know what I saw."

"I know," Nick affirmed.

Kay glanced in the rearview mirror. The sky was still empty.

She drove the Jeep down the road toward her apartment.

The second Kay left the woods, she was overcome with visions. Not surprisingly, Monday was a very stressful day for people.

Fortunately, at this point, she had ArrowVision pretty dialed in and was not debilitated by the rush of emotions and mental images.

Kay dropped her backpack and Shotgun off at her apartment. Carlo was still sleeping off his shift from the night before. He had agreed over text to walk Shotgun today so Kay could go straight from work to the Bicentennial Celebration.

Most of Kay's workdays were average. But, on this particular Monday, Kay got to experience the lives of her coworkers in a completely different way. It turned out that a lot of people didn't enjoy working at Mytherra. She felt and saw the anxiety of the people around her. On Friday, she had felt so alone, but now she felt a solidarity with these people—people she naively thought were corporate drones before.

The only person who surprised her was Harold. There wasn't any anxiety coming off that guy; he was so content with his life and being.

The fluorescent lights cast a pale, soulless glow over the rows of cubicles on Kay's floor. She spent most of the day staring at the little clock in the corner of her monitor. Her stomach churned with a mix of caffeine and s'mores Pop-Tarts. She clicked between tabs, pretending to work, until 5:00 p.m. rolled around.

The entire day was spent thinking about the Umbravue in the sky, ArrowVision, levitating, and their BlackHole break-in plan.

5:00 p.m. – Kay was out of there and on her way to meet Nick.

Chapter 40

5:21 p.m. – The parking lot at Bob's Corner Grocer was nearly empty; everyone was probably at the Bicentennial Celebration already.

Kay leaned against her old Cherokee, the engine still ticking softly as it cooled in the crisp air. Her breath curled in faint white wisps, dissipating into the stillness of the evening. She pulled her jacket tighter, her fingers fumbling with the zipper as the sharp chill of the wind bit at her cheeks and nose. The faint smell of burning wood from a nearby chimney and dry leaves hung in the air.

Her gaze drifted up toward the Bronco's headlights as it pulled into the lot; her heart skipped as Nick climbed out of the driver's side, grinning his mischievous smile.

"Hey," he said as he approached. He reached into his plaid jacket pocket, pulling out a single candy bar.

It was one of the marshmallow, rainbow sprinkle, milk chocolate bars Kay could only find at Shadowflight—Nick knew they were her favorite.

"Thank you," she blushed and put the candy in her pocket.

"You didn't have to wait out here in the cold."

"I was excited to see you," Kay admitted.

"You're freezing," he whispered, wrapping his arms around her and pulling her close. She rested her head against his chest, his warmth radiating through the layers of their jackets.

"I'm sorry I'm a couple of minutes late. We had to get things organized at the shop since Jimmy will be gone for a few weeks," Nick explained, still squeezing her.

"I totally understand," Kay assured. She felt a pang of sadness as a flashback to finding Jimmy the day before came to mind.

"Are you ready to do this?" Nick asked, seriously now, looking Kay straight in the eyes, unflinching.

"Yes." Kay was ready to get some answers.

"Do you think you have ArrowVision figured out enough to hang out at the celebration and act normal without getting too overwhelmed?"

"Yes," Kay answered, unwavering.

Chapter 41

The Owlsbourne Town Square was brimming with town pride. Families strolled hand in hand, bundled in coats and scarves, their breath visible in the brisk, clear November air. The square was transformed into a celebration of history. Booths lined the perimeter, offering local products like jars of honey with hand-lettered labels, baskets of apples from nearby orchards, and hand-stitched quilts. The centerpiece of the celebration was the Owlsbourne Meetinghouse, its white clapboard exterior illuminated by spotlights, proudly standing as it had for centuries.

Near the meetinghouse steps, a group of reenactors in colonial clothes performed a skit about the town's founding. A brass band stood on display in the town gazebo and played a mix of patriotic songs. Hung across the top of the gazebo was a large Allerzil banner that read, "Allerzil—Relief that's worth celebrating!"

Couples danced beneath strings of lights, while others stood on the sidelines, sipping steaming hot cider or mulled wine served in commemorative bicentennial mugs — mugs supplied by BlackHole, the event sponsor. The smell of roasted chestnuts and freshly baked pies filled the air.

Kay and Nick walked over from the grocery store, where they had parked their cars.

Kay immediately spotted Harold, Florence, and their son, Scout.

"Kay!" Harold waved as he ran over, the mulled wine sloshing out of his commemorative mug. Florence and Scout followed him. Florence was effortlessly beautiful, as usual. She had the timeless beauty of someone who looked like they belonged in an old photograph—soft, natural features framed by loose waves of red hair.

Kay was already bombarded by visions of people from around the event, but as Florence approached, she saw Florence's perspective.

Why Florence? She always seems so happy. She and Harold have a great relationship.

"Hi, Kay! Hi, Nick!" Florence greeted each of them with a one-armed hug while holding Scout's hand with her green, leather-gloved hand.

"Hey, buddy!" Nick gave Scout a fist pump. "How is your new bow working out?"

"It's great!" Scout answered, smiling from ear to ear.

"Thanks again for setting him up with that, Nick. I know absolutely nothing about archery, but this guy wanted to learn, and we knew Shadowflight was the place," Harold thanked Nick as he took a sip from his mug.

"Anytime," Nick smiled.

Kay wondered why Florence was so anxious. She watched as Florence tugged at the lapel of her black wool coat while her eyes darted around the town square.

Kay could see Florence's perspective through ArrowVision, but right now, all she could see through Florence's eyes was her and Nick standing there.

Kay glanced around the crowd. She noticed her family—Bruce, Pam, Luke, and Zoey, with her husband and kids. She saw Siren Hex talking with the Owlsbourne mayor. She saw Fred, her boss, chatting up the new, young secretary he had just hired. She spotted Jonny Langley on the outskirts, sitting on a memorial bench reading a book, and Penny's parents across the town green sharing funnel cake.

Wow—everyone is here, Kay thought to herself.

Nick gently tugged at her sleeve. "Want to go say hi to your family?"

"Sure." Kay didn't want her family to think that she and Nick were an item. She didn't need their pestering or their snide remarks. She and Nick agreed not to show affection toward each other in public; they didn't need people asking questions about anything they were up to. Still, Kay knew her mom, Pam, would be all over it. Pam's singular dream for her daughter was for Kay to find a good man. She would be thrilled to see Kay accompanied by any guy.

"Sure," Kay relented.

"We'll catch up with you guys more in a few," Kay hugged Florence again and slapped Scout a high five.

"Sure thing!" Harold eagerly agreed.

Chapter 42

Kay and Nick walked toward the McQuinn family.

The moment Pam caught a glimpse of Nick, she grinned.

"Ohhhh, did you two come together?" Pam ended the question on a high note.

"No, no, we just saw each other and started talking about archery stuff," Kay immediately rebutted.

"Right," Pam shrugged, surely disappointed that Kay had more "guy stuff" in common with Nick than most other guys. "Well, did you try on the sweater I got you for your birthday? Also, Cynthia called me; she said you haven't responded to the Baking Belles' invitation that she sent you. Kay, you need to be more respectfu—"

Before Pam could lecture Kay in front of everyone, Bruce, Kay's dad, jumped in, "I'm sure Cynthia can wait a couple more days." He smiled, softening the mood, reading Kay's very annoyed expression.

"Oh, sure. Just please call her, Kay. The ladies would love to have you involved in some local events," Pam persisted. "The ladies" were all the women in town who enjoyed clubs like *The Baking Belles* and *The Book & Biscuit Club* and who longed to gossip about so-and-so's new, ugly, expensive window treatments.

"Hey, Nick! How are things at the shop? I miss stopping by," Bruce assertively grabbed and shook Nick's hand.

The sight of Kay's father made her sad. The drinking was ruining him. His eyes were sunken, and his skin was pale and clammy.

Nick, always polite, smiled. "It's great! We have to get your bow set up and get you back out hunting, Mr. McQuinn."

"I'd love to get out in the woods again. Kay has been showing me trailcam photos of some epic bucks out on my mom's property. I just haven't had any time. Work is so busy."

"I totally get it. Well, I'll be at Shadowflight whenever you're ready," Nick offered.

Luke interrupted, not even pretending to be interested in the conversation. "Hi, Kay," he said dismissively. He rushed, "I'm going to go chat with Sarah over at the caramel popcorn stand. She's a world traveler, so I'm sure we have plenty to talk about—especially being stuck in this boring town. It was nice meeting you, Mick." Getting Nick's name wrong.

Before anyone responded, Luke was gone. He had met Nick about a thousand other times in his life, but he wasn't interested in the details of people who didn't benefit him or listen to his stories.

"Zoey was just here, but I think she and Matt took their kids to the inflatable slide next to the bank," Bruce kept the conversation moving.

"Okay, cool, well, I think we're going to walk around a bit and grab some of that mulled wine."

"Sounds good. See you soon, kiddo," Bruce hugged his daughter tight, and then Pam kissed Kay on the cheek and whispered in her ear.

"Nick is really cute—go for it!" Then she winked at Kay.

Kay flushed.

Then she spun around quickly and pulled Nick with her as they walked toward the mulled wine stand to get their BlackHole commemorative mugs.

Chapter 43

Kay pulled her coat tighter around her torso and shoved her free hand into her coat pocket. The other hand held her mulled wine, and her breath puffed out in soft clouds. Beside her, Nick juggled a steaming cup of cider in one hand and a bag of roasted chestnuts in the other.

They wandered around the town square for a little while. She used ArrowVision but didn't see anything suspicious— not even with Siren Hex, who was still mingling with the town mayor while holding her daughter, Veronica, near her to keep her warm. Siren's daughter looked like she might be around fourteen years old. Kay wondered what it was like to have one of the most influential people in the world as a mom.

"I think this cider might be boiling," Nick said, wincing as he blew on the surface of the cup. "Seeing anything interesting?"

"No, not really," Kay admitted. "I need to get my dad's BlackHole keycard, and we can go. He always keeps it in the glove box of his Beemer."

They kept wandering. As they walked by the mayor and Siren, Siren looked directly at Kay, about ten yards away, and gave her a smile and a nod. Kay, unsure of what to do, smiled back. Then, Siren went back to chatting people up.

The exchange was fast and weird. Nick thought so, too.

"What was that?" Nick elbowed Kay's side.

"I have no idea. I mean, I've met Siren before. She is my dad's boss, but why did she wave and nod at me?"

"Yeah, that was strange," Nick agreed as they meandered further.

"Do you think she knows we were outside the QuikCash the other day?" Kay worried.

"No, no way. Plus, even if we were, it's not like she would know that we know anything," Nick assured. "I think she was just being cordial to an employee's family member."

"Okay," Kay accepted, but something about the exchange was unsettling.

A makeshift stage had been set up near the town hall. The Owlsbourne mayor, a portly man with an impressive mustache and a less impressive ability to hold an audience's attention, stepped up to the microphone. He cleared his throat; the feedback from the speakers elicited a collective flinch from the crowd.

"Oh, no," Kay whispered, leaning closer to Nick. "It's happening. Mayor Thornwell is going to give one of his speeches. Take a sip every time he thanks BlackHole, says 'sense of community,' looks out at the crowd in panic, or reads from his note cards."

"Deal," Nick laughed. "You'll be drunk by the end of his speech."

"Yeah, probably not a good game to play right now," Kay retracted her suggestion.

As the speech dragged on, Kay and Nick wandered toward the edge of the square, drawn by the smell of sugared donuts frying at one of the stands. Kay bought a bag, and they ate as they walked; powdered sugar dusted their hands.

By the time the mayor finally concluded, the two of them were perched on the edge of the stone wall bordering the town square, watching the crowd disperse.

"I'll go grab my dad's car keys. I'll make up some reason I have to get into his car. Then I'll grab the BlackHole keycard and meet you back here," Kay strategized.

"Sounds good," Nick agreed. "I'll hang tight and polish off these donuts." Then Nick gently squeezed Kay's hand— subtly, so no one around would notice.

With that, she hopped off the ledge and walked straight toward her dad on the other side of the square.

Chapter 44

As Kay walked across the town square, ArrowVision flickered in and out of her head. She had pretty good control of the power by now.

Then she noticed Florence's green leather gloves flicker by in her mind, so she decided to tune in. It would only take a second.

Kay sat on one of the white banquet fold-out chairs scattered on the town green.

In Kay's mind, she saw two leather green–gloved hands holding a crappy flip phone—like the kind of phone that a college weed dealer might carry around. The same leather-gloved right hand that was holding Scout's hand just an hour earlier was now furiously texting.

Kay could feel Florence's emotional rollercoaster—a suffocating mix of shame, anxiety, and exhilaration.

There was no name at the top of the text thread, like smartphones have now, but Kay could read the texts through Florence's eyes.

Florence: *I love you. I want more than this.*

Unknown Number: *You know I can't give you more.*

Florence: *Why not? What's keeping you? You told me you don't even love your wife. You're just going to stay miserable forever? That's your plan?*

Unknown Number: *It's not about being miserable. It's about keeping things together for my family. I've told you this.*

Florence: *Do you even care about what I want? What we could have?*

Unknown Number: *I can't think about that right now. I can't think about us.*

Florence: *Then maybe I should stop waiting for you to figure it out. I deserve more than breadcrumbs, Fred.*

Florence's eyes, moist with tears, looked up from the phone screen toward the caramel apple stand. She shoved the burner phone in her coat pocket.

"Hey, buddy! All set?" Florence reached out her hand to Scout, who must have been buying the fresh caramel apple he was now gnawing on. "Let's go find Dad!"

In a blink, Kay sat back in the white fold-out chair, twenty yards away from her parents. She scanned the town square and spotted Florence and Scout walking away from the caramel apple stand. Scout's caramel apple, now half-eaten, stuck to his hand where the caramel had melted and dripped.

Then Scout's sticky hand dropped the caramel apple as it reached for his loving dad, Harold, in a sweet embrace. Florence stood a few feet back as her happy family enjoyed the town celebration, unaware of her affair.

Chapter 45

"Oh, Harold…" Kay said quietly to no one.

How would she tell him? Should she confront Florence?

She didn't have time to think about that right now. Her parents were about to walk away, and she needed to get her dad's keys ASAP.

Then, Kay saw a barred owl sitting on a light post, like the one she had seen Saturday morning. It turned its head, looked at her, and flew off.

She stood up and walked toward her parents.

"Hey, Dad! Wait up!"

Bruce was walking away toward—Kay already knew—the mulled wine stand. "I think I dropped one of my AirPods in your car last week when we got lunch. I've looked everywhere else for it and can't find it anywhere. Can I have your keys to check really quick before I head out?"

"Of course, kiddo—here you go."

Bruce tossed Kay the keys. "We'll be over at the mulled wine stand. I actually parked near there—we'll walk with you."

"Okay!"

Kay, her mom, and her dad walked together. Bruce had that familiar glassiness in his eyes as he rambled on about work and colleagues Kay didn't know. Kay wondered to herself how long he had been off the wagon. Though Pam tried to conceal it as she smiled through Bruce's babbling, Kay saw the pain in her mom's eyes. Pam was from a generation of women who stuck by their men, no matter what. So, all these years, Pam just smiled and nodded along as her husband drifted in and out of alcoholism.

As they approached the mulled wine, Bruce pointed to a side street about fifteen yards past the stand. "My car is parked right over there! We'll wait for you here." He grinned, his fatherly-loving grin, as they got in line for more wine. Despite his flaws, Kay loved her dad so much; he was one of her best friends.

"Sounds good," Kay answered as she walked toward the side street.

As soon as she turned the corner, she spotted the sapphire-blue BMW. When she pressed unlock on the keychain, the car beeped open.

Kay knew that, despite better judgment, Bruce kept his BlackHole keycard in the glove box of his car. He was always carefree, and he got even sloppier with everything when he was drinking.

Kay slid into the passenger side, the black leather seats cold from the night air.

ArrowVision was still very active in her mind. However, it had sort of become a television automatically cycling through channels in the far back of her brain. In short, ArrowVision had become background noise unless she felt the need to "tune in."

"Gotcha," Kay grabbed the keycard from the glove box. Bruce was nothing if not a totally predictable dad.

As Kay was about to climb out of the BMW with the keycard in hand, she had a vision of her father's perspective. She saw her mom standing only a few feet away in the mulled wine line and recognized the hook-shaped scar on his right hand.

Why was her dad so nervous? She felt his anxiety. His body felt extra hot in his black wool coat. He was texting a message to Siren Hex; Siren's name, with a small headshot, was at the top of the iPhone conversation. This was not unusual, since Siren was Bruce's boss. Kay read the messages.

Siren: *Please, Bruce.*

Bruce: *I know you want more marketing designs, but I can't take any more of Kay's artwork. I feel so guilty about recommending her artwork for Allerzil. I know we needed a great marketing campaign to raise funding and keep our jobs—but we're good now, aren't we? I just can't...*

His shaking hands typed the last letters on his iPhone and moved to hit "send."

In a blink, Kay was back in the Beemer, crying.

Chapter 46

It was her dad who stole her art. The thought screamed in her mind.

It was him.

Kay sat in the car, paralyzed. Tears streamed down her cheeks. The makeup she had so carefully applied to look extra cute for Nick was streaked and smudged. The truth slashed through her mind like a blade, unraveling years of trust instantly. Her breath was short; her fingers trembled as they clutched at the fabric of her coat. She squeezed her wolf necklace out of habit.

How could she have missed it? How could her dad steal her art?

Kay was at a loss. She was devastated. Her heart ached with betrayal and grief. She knew her parents had money problems a few years back, but stealing her art to keep his job seemed despicably low. Her mind raced back to every moment, every word he had ever spoken to her. How many lies were there?

When she thought about it more, she remembered other poor, alcohol-induced decisions Bruce had made over the years. There was never a time in Kay's life when Bruce's job didn't come before his family.

And Siren's involvement did not surprise Kay at all. Siren Hex was cutthroat and dishonest. Kay already *knew* that.

Kay lost her career. And her love of art. Kay lost herself. She had no money. She was suicidal. She was lonely and defeated. There were mornings she couldn't get out of bed, and nights she didn't want to see the next day. All because of him. All because of her own father and his selfishness.

Bruce had watched Kay struggle these last few years, knowing he had caused it. Now, Kay knew why he was always offering her a job and money. He felt guilty.

Kay decided not to confront Bruce tonight. Getting in a fight with her dad right now would ruin her plan to break into BlackHole. She would be distracted. Despite her anger, she had to stay composed. Kay swallowed hard and straightened, forcing the weight of her emotions into a quiet simmer. ArrowVision helped a little bit to keep her calm.

Why doesn't it just solve my stress? The calming and meditative effects of ArrowVision seemed selective.

Kay pulled down the mirror in the Beemer and fixed her streaky makeup. Then, she hid the keycard in her coat pocket and walked back to the mulled wine stand.

Kay approached the man she had admired only minutes before. He had been her protector, her supporter, her friend.

"No luck!" She tossed Bruce the keys and choked back a lump in her throat. "Thanks for letting me look. I'm going to go find Nick!"

"Okay, kiddo." Bruce wrapped his arm around Pam's side.

"Have fun with Nick," Pam winked suggestively. Before her parents could say anything more, Kay turned and walked away, concealing the tears in her eyes.

"Hey!" Nick's expression softened when he spotted Kay walking toward him.

Before he could say anything else, Kay wrapped her arms around him.

She pressed her forehead into his shoulder and squeezed her eyes shut. The warmth—Nick's steady heartbeat against her own—only worsened the ache.

"Are you okay?" A soft whisper.

Kay didn't speak. She couldn't. If she did, the dam would break, and she wasn't sure if she could put herself back together.

Nick said nothing.

Kay and Nick stood there for just a moment, embracing, shutting out the world and its ugliness. Kay didn't care who saw them together anymore. She held onto Nick tighter, as if squeezing him would keep the grief from swallowing her whole.

Chapter 47

8:23 p.m. – The car ride back to Kay's apartment was a blur. After their hug, Kay and Nick only said a few words to each other. Kay wasn't ready to share what she had discovered about her dad; she was embarrassed, and Nick didn't pry. She didn't want to think about it. They left Kay's Jeep at the grocery store for now.

In the Bronco, Kay leaned in just enough for her breath to tickle Nick's ear. "Drive faster."

Her roommate, Carlo, was working, and Kay knew it.

They stumbled into Kay's apartment. Nick's wet lips pressed against Kay's in a deep and consuming kiss. His hands mapped out the curve of her waist, pressing her flush against him.

Nick pulled Kay's head back by her hair and kissed her neck as she unbuckled his belt.

10:04 p.m. – "I guess we better get ourselves ready for this mission," Nick suggested, tracing the arch of Kay's back with his fingertips. His forehead glistened as he leaned in to kiss her bare shoulder. "Can I see your other shoulder?" he asked gently.

She rolled over in the sheets, revealing a red, spiral arrow clearly branded into her shoulder. The mark was no longer a welt or raised. It looked almost like a tattoo, but of course, with no ink—just scarring.

"Wow," Nick whispered. "Can I touch it?"

"Go ahead."

He carefully placed his first finger on the outside of the spiral, where the arrowhead was visible. "Does it hurt?"

"Not anymore," Kay answered.

Nick exhaled and rolled onto his back, staring at the ceiling. He asked, "Are you okay? I don't expect you to tell me everything, but as your boyfriend, I want you to feel comfortable talking to me."

Kay propped herself up on her elbows. "Boyfriend?" She smiled as she said it.

"I mean, if you'll have me. I want to be with you, Kay. I don't want to date anyone else, and I don't want you to date anyone either." Nick knew what he wanted.

A warmth rose in Kay's cheeks. Her eyes flicked downward for a moment, then back up. A soft, breathy laugh escaped her lips. "Sure."

Nick laughed out loud. "Sure?! Well, I'll take it!"

It was clear that Kay was more than smitten with Nick, but "sure" was all she thought to say. The craziness of the night left her without words.

Nick put his hands around Kay's jaw, his gaze lingering on her, softly, reverently. He kissed her cheek. His lips barely touched her skin, the warmth of which lingered, sending a gentle shiver through Kay. He moved slowly, pressing another kiss to her temple, then one at the corner of her mouth, savoring the quiet closeness between them. His breath was steady, his touch tender, strong but safe. Then, they rolled back into the sheets.

That was much better than thinking about her fucked-up life.

10:42 p.m. – Kay and Nick took Shotgun for a long walk before heading to BlackHole.

"Want to tell me now why you've been so quiet since the Bicentennial celebration?" Nick wrapped his arm around Kay's waist, pulling her close, as they walked Shotgun down a narrow path between apartment buildings.

"I think it'll make me cry if I say it out loud."

Nick stopped. "Make you cry? I don't like that." He was in protector mode again.

Kay turned to look at him, her lips trembling. Her eyes glistened. Her voice wavered as she held back tears. "Umm, well, you know how BlackHole stole my art a few years ago?" Kay had told Nick about everything one day when she was at Shadowflight.

"Oh, yeah, how could I forget? That place is really something else." He was much angrier than Kay expected him to be.

"When I was near my parents earlier, I got a flash of my dad's phone, through ArrowVision, and he was texting Siren Hex about how he was the one who gave BlackHole my art for the Allerzil ad." A single tear trailed down her cheek.

"Wait, your dad gave BlackHole your original art without you knowing?" Nick sounded disgusted and confused all at once.

"It would seem so," Kay choked out.

"Why?" Nick asked, though he knew there was no real, justifiable answer to that question.

Kay stared blankly, tears now rolling down her cheeks. "He was texting something about him needing to keep his job. I know he's had money problems in the past. It seemed like Siren was pressuring him to get more art out of me or something."

"Well, that's beyond shitty," Nick said matter-of-factly as he wrapped Kay in a hug. "I'm sorry. Your dad doesn't seem like he would do something like that. He seems so... loving..."

"It's okay. I don't want to talk about it, or even think about it right now," Kay muttered into Nick's chest.

"Okay," he held her.

They didn't say much after that. They finished their walk, Shotgun's leash pulled taut as he tugged them forward, tail wagging, oblivious to the gloomy tone the night had now taken on.

Back at Kay's apartment, Nick and Kay got dressed in black clothes. They tried to imagine what burglars might wear in a situation like this. Except Kay's shirt had neon pink *Kings of Leon* letters plastered across the front, and Nick's had the Shadowflight Archery logo. They grabbed silver duct tape that was in Kay's apartment and stuck it over any shirt graphics. Hopefully, cameras wouldn't catch them… but if the cameras did, they didn't need to give themselves away entirely.

Kay and Nick also had extra big black beanies that Nick snagged from work before leaving that day. They cut holes in the beanies for eyes and slits for their mouths. They made sure that their phones were charged, and Kay double-checked that she had the BlackHole keycard. She figured Bruce wouldn't notice the keycard was gone tonight; he'd be too buzzed on mulled wine. She just needed to put it back in his car before work in the morning.

Chapter 48

TUESDAY

12:22 a.m. – The BlackHole headquarters loomed in the darkness like a concrete monster, devoid of warmth or any sign of human life. The building was a five-level fortress of reinforced steel and glass, with thick, tinted windows. Security cameras sat at each corner of the building, watching the sidewalks, big-brother style. Surprisingly, there was no security fence surrounding the building. No security fence had been part of BlackHole's "community integration" effort. The company thought that security fences and gates would separate the building from the town of Owlsbourne. They claimed that no fences made the headquarters more "approachable" to the community.

The building embodied a world that Kay hated—an ugly, drab box filled with technology and people determined to make a profit at all costs. It had no heart or character; it was a product of greed and corruption. The building cast a dark shadow on the once farm-centered, quaint town of Owlsbourne.

She and Nick stood behind a tree across the street. They had parked the Bronco up the road in a commuter lot and walked over to BlackHole.

"Are you ready to do this?" he whispered to her. "We can't go back after this." Finally, after being so stoic all weekend, Nick sounded hesitant. Kay could see his perspective in the back of her mind through ArrowVision. He was extremely nervous, though his face, as always, was calm. His eyes were kind and concerned.

Kay brought her face close to his. She didn't feel nervous anymore; she didn't have panic attacks.

Her lips hovered an inch from Nick's.

"We got this. Something is going on, and we are going to figure it out." Then Kay laughed just a little. "Or we'll be in a shitload of trouble."

Before Nick said anything, she kissed him, his stubble tickling her chin as she wrapped her arms around him.

"Thank you for everything." She held him tight. "Thank you for believing in me."

"Kay McQuinn, I have always, *always* believed in you. Let's do this." He smiled, stepped back, and pulled the cut-up black beanie over his face. In his black burglar outfit, Nick faded into the dark night—of course, except for the silver duct tape across his chest.

Their entire plan relied on the promise of some internet message board person. Breaking into BlackHole was reckless. Kay knew that, and Nick did too. But Kay was so tired of not knowing what was going on. If she lost her mind, she might as well go down in a blaze. And Nick was so enamored by Kay, he didn't really care what happened, as long as he was with her.

Kay led the way as she and Nick quietly and discreetly made their way to the south side of the building.

Just as they reached the south side entrance, they saw a security guard emerge from the front door of the building and light a cigarette. The guard was oblivious to their existence—*not much of a guard*, Kay thought. He took a slow drag and leaned against the concrete wall. Standing in the middle of a perfectly manicured flower bed, he exhaled a stream of smoke into the night.

Kay pulled out Bruce's keycard and gingerly swiped it. The door gave a soft click, and Kay eased it open. They slipped inside. The hallway's overhead lights were dim.

Nick set a timer on his watch as he pulled Kay's sleeve. "We've got nine minutes before the guard comes back and security is live—according to the tipster, anyway."

Kay nodded. They moved as one, silent as ghosts, through the bleak, dark corridor until they reached the corner office on the left.

They reached Siren's office, marked by a beautiful bronze placard on the wall next to the doorframe: *Siren Hex, Chief*

Executive Officer. Kay recognized the keypad on Siren's door from watching her dad unlock his office over the years. Kay glanced at her wrist, just below the line of her glove, where she had written the code from the tipster with a ballpoint pen.

Kay's fingers punched into the keypad: five-six-eight-three-four.

Red light.

She muttered a curse.

"Come on, come on…"

She tried again. This time, the light turned green with a faint click.

They ducked inside.

"Seven minutes," Nick whispered as they looked around for the owl that the internet tipster had mentioned.

Inside, the room was illuminated by the bluish glow of a neon tube sign on the far wall that read *Wiring Minds For Tomorrow*, in script lettering. The light flickered and rotated to a new neon color every ten seconds or so. In the center of the square room was a commanding oak desk. The office was stark, organized, and soulless—just like Siren. On the desk were neatly stacked reports, a leather notebook, a framed school photo of Siren's daughter, and an old cup of coffee in a disposable paper cup.

Then, Kay spotted it. Just behind the black conference phone on the desk was a gray, ceramic figurine of an owl, only about six inches tall.

"Look." Kay gestured toward the owl to Nick, who was standing and looking over her shoulder.

He followed as Kay very carefully lifted the owl.

Sure enough, underneath the figurine was a small key that looked like it was for a chest or cabinet, not a door.

File name "SEE", Kay thought. Her eyes darted around the room. Nick was already stepping over to a black file cabinet in the back corner, behind the desk.

The file cabinet had two large drawers. It was as average as they come, with no special locks, symbols, or security. Kay wondered, for a moment, if this internet tipster was messing with them.

She knelt next to Nick, who was already investigating the cabinet's sturdiness. He looked at his watch.

"Five minutes," Nick warned, sounding anxious.

"Okay, okay," Kay said as she tried the key in the lock. As she turned the key, the drawers fell open.

She and Nick started rifling through the file tab names. Most of the files were typical—monthly reports and stuff like that. But then, at the very back of the bottom drawer, Kay spotted the word *SEE*. Kay ripped out the file and began skimming, knowing she had mere seconds to scan the documents inside before they had to leave.

[CONFIDENTIAL]

INTERNAL MEMORANDUM
PROJECT: SEE
CLEARANCE LEVEL: DEEP-BLACK
FILE NO: 903-XT-77
DATE: [REDACTED]
AUTHORIZED PERSONNEL ONLY

TO: [REDACTED], Executive Board

FROM: Dr. Siren Hex, Director of Bio-Technological Innovations DEEP-BLACK

SUBJECT: Phase III Human Trials - "SEE" Initiative

EXECUTIVE SUMMARY:
As of [REDACTED], **Phase III trials of the SEE Initiative** have yielded **significant breakthroughs** in cognitive augmentation, neural integration, and **prototype deployment** of the [REDACTED] interface. However, **unforeseen biological degradation** in test subjects has necessitated additional revisions. **Projected commercial viability remains intact,** provided containment and disposal protocols are maintained. Ability to harness Umbravue powers appears probable.

SECTION 1: EXPERIMENTAL FINDINGS

Test subjects have exhibited the following post-integration results:

✓ **Phase I-III: Neural Synchronization** - **87% success rate** in establishing baseline synaptic connectivity.

✓ **Phase II: Cognitive Enhancement** - Temporary ability to view others' perspectives with the mind. Subjects report new feelings of calm, peace, and happiness.

✗ **Phase III: Structural Integrity Failure** - **100% fatality rate** due to **cerebral hemorrhaging, cardiac arrest, or systemic collapse** within **72 hours of ingesting metallic pill.**

Post-mortem analysis reveals that **the metallic compound does not degrade post-mortem,** suggesting potential **long-term bioaccumulation risks.** Further testing is required to determine whether the **pill is modifying neural architecture beyond intended parameters.**

Despite these outcomes, the data confirms the **potential viability** of the SEE technology. Modifications to **Version 4.7 of the neural interface** are currently in progress to mitigate terminal failures.

SECTION 2: DECEASED TEST SUBJECTS (PHASE III MORTALITY LOG)

NAME	AGE	STATUS	CAUSE OF DEATH
Stan McQinn	71	Deceased	Cardiac Arrest
Maria Lenz	28	Deceased	Neural Overload – Stroke
Elena Vasquez	34	Deceased	Systemic Collapse
David Cho	41	Deceased	Organ Failure
Marcus Knight	45	Deceased	Cerebral Hemorrhage
Unknown (NPR-22)	??	Deceased	Seizure-Induced Coma
Unknown (NPR-77)	??	Deceased	Multi-System Collapse
James Calloway	39	Deceased	Sudden Systemic Failure

Tasha King	62	Deceased	Neural Degeneration
Penny Grant	21	Deceased	Cerebral Aneurysm
Unknown (NPR-98)	??	Deceased	Respiratory Failure
Hannah Reddington	29	Deceased	Cardiac Arrest
Simon Patel	38	Deceased	Neural Disintegration
Adam Reese	26	Deceased	Systemic Organ Collapse

Total Fatalities: 14

Note: Subjects were procured via **[REDACTED]** and remain **untraceable** in official records.

SECTION 3: ETHICAL & LEGAL LIABILITY MITIGATION

To ensure **discretion and operational security,** all Phase III subjects have been designated as

"Non-Registered Participants" (NRPs), eliminating traceability.

Protocol 77 (Terminal Event Containment):

- **Immediate disposal** via site at casino - contingency in case bodies need exhumation for further analysis.
- **Data Anonymization Directive:** Erasure of all test subject records within **48 hours** of termination.
- **Media & Public Risk Containment:** Implementation of standard misinformation procedures in the event of unauthorized exposure.

Corporate Legal Advisory confirms that as long as containment remains **airtight**, external accountability remains **low-risk**.

SECTION 4: NEXT STEPS & RECOMMENDATIONS

1. **Initiate Phase IV Trials** with modified neural dampeners to counteract system overload.
2. **Increase Subject Pool Acquisition** via [REDACTED] facilities.
3. **Enhance PR Countermeasures** in case of external scrutiny - deploy pre-prepared narrative of **"unfounded allegations"** should leaks occur.
4. **Full Market Readiness Projection: Q4 [REDACTED]** (contingent on adjusted mortality rates).

The **board must approve the extension of human trials within the next 72 hours** to maintain timeline integrity. Non-compliance will result in automatic escalation to **DEEP-BLACK** Contingency.

Signed,
Dr. Siren Hex
Director, Bio-Technological Innovations DEEP-BLACK
[REDACTED CORPORATION NAME]

ATTACHED FILES:

1. Mortality Report: Subject 003-027
2. Phase III Brainwave Data - Classified
3. DEEP-BLACK-77 Disposal Confirmation Logs

WARNING: UNAUTHORIZED ACCESS WILL BE PROSECUTED TO FULL EXTENT OF CORPORATE LAW

Kay's hands shook as her eyes quickly scanned over the file repeatedly. Piled behind the initial report were stacks of in-depth findings. The files weren't just research logs. They were death certificates. Autopsy reports. Surveillance footage. Subject after subject—human test subjects—alive, thinking, feeling people—had been fed that pill. The orange, metallic, triangle pill Kay had seen through ArrowVision at the QuikCash just days before.

Kay's pulse hammered against her ribs. She read the deceased names in the "SEE" file: Stan McQuinn, Marcus Knight, and Penny Grant. She gagged, clamping a hand over her mouth as bile burned the back of her throat. Her stomach lurched.

Kay's pupils were wide with disbelief. She had forgotten how to breathe. She could feel cold sweat beading at her temple. Her skin crawled as if she could feel the dead clawing at her, whispering, demanding she do something.

Nick, always calm—on the outside at least—quietly scanned the file over Kay's shoulder. Without even acknowledging the horror he was witnessing, he said, "Three minutes. We need to go, Kay!"

Kay was frozen. She was overcome with grief. According to this document, BlackHole had killed her grandfather, her boyfriend's dad, and her best friend. She touched the wolf necklace that still hung around her neck.

Was Nick reading the same document she was? How was he not more upset?

Finally, Nick took the file from Kay's motionless hands.

He laid the papers on the desk and began snapping photos with his phone.

"Kay, I know this is fucked up, but we have to get out of here," he reminded, nervously re-stacking the papers into the file folder and placing it back in the back of the small filing cabinet.

He buzzed around Kay, locking the file cabinet and putting the key back under the owl figurine, as she sat on the floor, paralyzed.

"Two minutes!" Nick shouted in a hushed yell as he grabbed Kay's elbow and pulled her to the door.

She snapped back to reality as they carefully shut the office door and snuck back down the corridor toward the exit.

Kay's heart was pounding so loudly, she was sure it would give them away. Behind her, she could hear Nick's shallow, sharp breathing. His hand was clamped around his phone, which held all the photos—and all the truth.

There were no alarms or flashing lights—not yet, anyway. The internet tipster had pulled through.

Then they heard boots, faint but close. Too close.

Nick grabbed Kay's arm and yanked her into a narrow alcove off the hallway.

A flashlight beam passed within inches of their hiding spot. Two guards. Quiet murmurs between them.

"… must've been a glitch."

"… motion sensor flicked for half a second."

Nick's grip tightened on Kay's sleeve. The flashlight moved again.

Then, Kay used ArrowVision to tune into the nervous guard's perspective. She could see which direction the guards were walking. She watched through ArrowVision as the guard's eyes glanced at Siren's office placard as he marched by. Then his boots took a right down the hallway leading away from Kay and Nick.

Kay exhaled. "Let's go," she mouthed as she led Nick confidently away from the guards on duty.

Kay and Nick reached the south-side exit. They slipped out of the EXIT door, and then they ran.

They crossed the street just before they saw the green power lights of several outdoor security cameras flicker back on.

Kay spun around to look at Nick, who was now bent over a bush. His body convulsed as his stomach rejected everything inside it.

Kay placed a hand on his back for comfort. He continued to retch. Eventually, he looked up with watery eyes and, in a scary tone that Kay had never heard before, he growled, "These people killed my dad," as he wiped his mouth with his sleeve.

"Yes," was all Kay could think to say.

The sight of throw-up made Kay gag, but she tried desperately to keep it together for Nick this time. He had been so supportive of her over the last few days. The least she could do at that moment was not freak out. Maybe she would save her freak-out for later. Though with ArrowVision, it seemed, she didn't feel the dread and panic like she used to.

"I mean... did we find what I think we just found?"

"I think we did," Kay answered, still at a loss for words.

Chapter 49

1:06 a.m. – Kay and Nick wanted to discuss their findings in the car, immediately, but decided the best course of action would be to review everything in the safety of Kay's apartment.

Nick dropped Kay off where she had parked her Jeep in the Bob's Grocer parking lot before the Bicentennial Celebration earlier. She immediately drove over to her parents' house to return Bruce's BlackHole keycard before morning, while Nick went to Kay's apartment to walk Shotgun and wait for Kay to return.

Her headlights illuminated the long, winding driveway that snaked up to the McQuinn house. Kay's fifteen-minute drive to her parents' felt like an eternity. She pulled the Jeep over several times on the way because she thought she would be sick.

Now, all she saw when looking at her dad's house was betrayal. In the craziness of BlackHole, Kay had forgotten, for a moment, about her father stealing her art.

She had spent all those years being upset and depressed over BlackHole, only to find out that her dad had caused all of it. He was the one who cost her her career. He watched her suffer and never said a thing. All the Christmases, birthdays, meals, and moments that they had shared were now distorted and ugly. He had betrayed her.

The worst part of the whole thing was that, deep down, Kay wasn't surprised. Throughout Kay's life, Bruce was who he was—not who Kay thought he was or wanted him to be. Bruce was someone who prioritized work, alcohol, and himself above all else.

How could she have been so stupid? So blind?

The McQuinn house looked different from when she was there last Friday night. Knowing what she knew now, the sight of the house made her disappointed and angry. It was a thing pretending to be something it wasn't—happiness, warmth, comfort—now contorted into deceit and greed. The windows were blank, empty eyes watching her pull up.

Kay knew the McQuinn garage door code, so she typed it into the keypad of the four-car garage and hit *enter.* The door cranked upward, and she ducked under it.

She figured Bruce would be too tipsy to lock his car when he got home, and that, in his alcohol-induced coma— something she had witnessed countless times—he would not notice Kay driving up the driveway and opening the garage in the middle of the night. Her mom slept with a mask and earplugs, so she knew she was safe there, too. And Luke… his life of privilege, peppered with a marijuana-induced high, allowed him a deep sleep most every night.

Kay was right about all of her assumptions. Her plan worked perfectly. No one came to see what was happening, and her dad left his car unlocked. She slipped the keycard back in the glove box, shut the garage, hopped in her Jeep, and headed home to Nick and Shotgun.

1:47 a.m. – Kay sat on the edge of the mattress in her apartment, her knee bouncing, eyes fixed on Nick's phone screen. The only lights in the cramped bedroom came from the glow of Kay's laptop screen, Nick's phone, and the neon flicker from the gas station across the street. Outside, the world was silent. Carlo was sleeping in the room on the other side of the paper-thin wall. Kay and Nick stayed quiet while Shotgun snored, louder than ever.

Nick leaned in over Kay's shoulder as she swiped through the many photos Nick snapped on his phone of the "SEE" file before they had to escape BlackHole. Each swipe revealed something worse than the last.

Confidential medical reports. Internal emails. Death certificates. Trial medications.

"Christ. This is disgusting," Nick muttered, his voice hoarse from exhaustion and puking in the parking lot.

Kay swiped to the list of deceased test subjects.

She read the names over and over: Stan McQuinn, Marcus Knight, and Penny Grant.

Her stomach twisted into knots. She was speechless. She was in shock.

Nick swallowed hard. "They killed my dad." His voice was shaking, but whether from rage or grief, Kay couldn't tell. Probably both. He was referring to his father, Marcus Knight, who everyone thought had died in a car accident.

Kay was empathetic to Nick but too distracted by her own loved ones' names: her grandfather, Stan McQuinn, and her best friend, Penny Grant. Kay had thought that Stan had died of a heart attack, and Penny had died of a drug overdose. Those things were partially true, it seemed, since Stan's death was listed as *Cardiac Arrest* and Penny's as *Cerebral Aneurysm.*

Kay's grip tightened on the phone. "They killed all of them." Her fingers dug into the fabric of her pants, her nails pressing hard into her skin. She couldn't take it anymore—it was too much.

Kay tried not to panic, but even the peace that seemed to come with ArrowVision couldn't curb the stress of these insane realizations. Kay ran to the bathroom—it was her turn to be sick.

A few minutes later, Kay gathered herself and joined Nick back on the mattress. They kept swiping, and there, at the very end, the last page of the stolen file, after several pages with redacted information, was a scanned Polaroid image of a black, tall, thin creature in a large test tube.

The creature drifted limply in a murky, orange-tinged liquid. A faded red spiral etched into its chest. Its sunken, sad, giant black eyes were unfocused and hazy with no recognition or understanding, just a dull, exhausted expression of hopelessness that hurt Kay's heart. The creature pressed one of its talons against the glass, as if silently begging the photographer to let it out.

Proudly standing next to the giant orange-slime tube was a younger Siren Hex. Her smug, cold eyes glared at the camera as she smiled, wearing a perfectly white lab coat. On the white of the Polaroid were the words *Umbravue Subject 00–01.*

Though the Polaroid scan was blurry, grainy, and visibly older than the rest of the pages in the file, Kay saw it perfectly. "Holy shit," Kay muttered. "That is an Umbravue. That is what I saw in the woods on Friday morning and yesterday morning in the sky."

The Polaroid was so damaged that, if you didn't know exactly what you were looking at, you couldn't see what it was a photo of.

"Are you sure? It's tough to make out," Nick said, squinting at the paper as he held it closer to his face.

"I'm positive." Kay was on her feet now. She was too anxious to stay seated.

"Okay, so BlackHole—specifically Siren Hex—has been testing an unapproved medication on random, unknowing subjects. Some of whom have been our family and friends."

Kay paced back and forth, beating a trail into the old gray apartment carpet, putting the puzzle together in her mind. "I saw through *ArrowVision* at the QuikCash the medication on Sunday, right after I found Jimmy in his truck. I saw Siren Hex, and I saw that squirrely guy holding a triangular, orange, metallic pill.”

She paused for a moment and froze.

“But! But… I couldn’t see clearly; everything was static, and then I lost the ArrowVision ‘signal.’” She used air quotes.

She paused for another moment, thinking, as Nick petted Shotgun and waited.

“The ArrowVision was static because that guy was taking the orange pill…” Then it dawned on her. “The orange pill is a synthetic form of ArrowVision!”

“That’s why BlackHole has information on the Umbravue. That’s why they have one in a test tube. They’re trying to replicate ArrowVision! Oh my God.”

Kay sat down, stunned. Staring at nothing.

“I think you’re right. That seems to be what this file says. But why? For the power of ArrowVision? Or the like…” Nick searched for words, “the ‘peace’ feeling that you describe comes with it? Or the levitating?”

“For all of it! It’s incredible. It’s revolutionary. And if BlackHole can harness ArrowVision and the other powers, it’ll change the world and make BlackHole an even bigger success. And Siren Hex… gosh, she would be like worshipped.”

“And really, who else knows what BlackHole has uncovered and what the Umbravue are capable of?” Nick added.

Kay noticed the tightness in Nick’s jaw. His hands trembled. What he felt was deeper than anger, and Kay felt it too. Fuck BlackHole. This company not only ruined her life, but it also killed their family members and her best friend.

Kay wanted a reckoning, and she knew Nick did too.

“We have to leak this.”

Kay sat beside Nick and held onto Shotgun’s paw for comfort.

Nick nodded. His clenched jaw softened a little.

He sat up straighter, his mind working. “Let’s post it online. Everywhere at once. Zeddit, Telegram, X. WikiLeaks.”

“Even if people claim it’s a hoax, it’ll at least bring attention to the issue. Let’s call in an anonymous tip to Owlsbourne PD about the bodies at the casino—the file must be referring to the construction site at The Golden Sphinx.”

“We have to do it *tonight*. I’m afraid, by tomorrow, someone will catch us for breaking into BlackHole. So, I think it’s now or never.”

"Okay, yeah. Let's do it." Nick leaned in and softly kissed Kay's lips.

Then he whispered, with a nervousness in his voice, "This is fucking crazy."

Chapter 50

3:42 a.m. – Kay's laptop screen glowed, illuminating their exhausted and still-shocked expressions. Kay had uploaded every document photo from the "SEE" file on Nick's phone to her laptop. She also backed up all the images to multiple USB drives.

The apartment was silent except for the faint hum of the fridge, Shotgun's snoring, and the distant sound of a car passing outside. Carlo was still asleep in the room next door, unaware that, right here, in this tiny, cramped bedroom, Kay and Nick were about to leak one of the biggest corporate scandals of the twenty-first century.

They had prepared everything. There were multiple upload points. The file photos were packed into compressed, encrypted folders, mirrored across different sites: WikiLeaks, Telegram, a dozen subZeddits, Discord servers, torrent networks, and anonymous forums. Each upload had been set to burners—disposable accounts that would vanish once the job was done. Kay knew nothing about this stuff, but apparently, Nick was pretty savvy and had learned a lot during his brief stint as a criminal.

As far as Kay's IP address was concerned, they had connected themselves to a VPN and were using the public Wi-Fi of the coffee shop next to Kay's apartment building. The signal was weak, but it was enough to upload images.

Kay's stomach twisted. Were they really going to do this? They had to. They couldn't ignore what they discovered. How many people were involved in this?

Nick reviewed their uploads. Then he looked over at Kay. "You ready?"

"I guess so. I don't think we have a choice."

"Do you want to do the honors?" he asked.

"Yes," Kay responded. "I got us into this. I want to *see* it through… pun intended." A bad joke that did not lighten the mood.

She placed her finger over the trackpad, hovering over the upload button. All the platforms were queued up so she could upload the images quickly to all of them.

Their eyes met in a silent confirmation.

"Three," Nick murmured.

"Two," Kay whispered.

She hit the upload button.

The progress bars flickered to life, filling slowly, then faster. Kay held her breath as the numbers climbed.

Twenty-five percent. Forty-two percent. Seventy-nine percent.

Then—Complete.

Kay let out a shaky breath. "It's done."

They sat there in silence, listening to the subtle tones of the apartment and the distant sound of a siren somewhere in Owlsbourne. The weight in their chests hadn't lifted; if anything, it felt heavier now.

Chapter 51

Kay and Nick sat on the mattress, watching their devices for as long as they could keep their eyes open. But by 4:40 a.m., with no activity on their posts about the leaked documents, they finally lay back, laptop between them, and dozed off.

Their posts hadn't taken off like wildfire. They got no traffic at all.

Kay drifted in and out of sleep; her night was anything but restful. Had all of this been for nothing? Had she selfishly dragged Nick into a compromising situation? But if all of this were true, then this company murdered innocent people. Maybe BlackHole would scrub it from the internet before anyone saw it. Who knew what they were capable of?

7:02 a.m. – "Kay, wake up." Nick shook her shoulder. The weight of exhaustion pulled at her eyelids. The bright light of morning stretched through the curtains, exposing Kay's meager, broke lifestyle in all its tattered glory.

Dust particles drifted in front of her eyes as she pried them open.

Nick had the laptop open, and a local news station's livestream was playing on the screen.

"Look," he said, sitting next to Kay and pulling the laptop closer between them as she groggily sat up.

Kay watched as the news reporter announced, "Breaking overnight: CEO of BlackHole, Siren Hex, has been taken into federal custody following an explosive leak of alleged confidential BlackHole documents. Authorities are now investigating multiple locations tied to the corporation, some possibly linked to long, unsolved missing persons cases. Police have begun searching for potential remains."

Ironically, an Allerzil ad banner scrolled below the news livestream.

Kay was awake now. "Shut the fuck up!" she shouted at Nick but stared at the screen, pulling it onto her lap.

"NO WAY!"

She watched as a stoic, fully dressed in a black pantsuit with a face full of makeup, Siren Hex was marched out of her Owlsbourne mansion in handcuffs. Reporters swarmed Siren, asking countless questions. She said nothing as the police placed her in the back of a cop car.

Nick reached for his phone. His eyes were bloodshot. "Holy shit," he muttered, staring at the screen. "It's everywhere."

He handed Kay the phone. Her hands shook as she scrolled through the flood of reactions. Journalists were dissecting the leak, social media was in a frenzy, and conspiracy theories were running wild.

The BlackHole scandal was the cover story on every single global news outlet.

"Holy shit, holy shit, holy shit," Kay got up, pacing and repeating in a hushed voice, cautious not to wake Carlo—mostly because she didn't want him to suspect anything unusual was happening in her room.

"What now?" Nick asked.

"I mean, I don't know," Kay answered honestly. "I guess if all our safety measures work, then no one can trace the leak to us, right?"

"Right," Nick affirmed.

"So, I guess we just go about our day and see how everything unravels? I don't want people to think we're acting suspiciously."

"Agreed," Nick said. Then he got up and walked over to Kay, who was pacing.

He grabbed her and held her in his arms. Then he whispered, "I know the last few days have been weird as hell. But I want you to know that you are so brave."

He kept holding her. "Despite the stuff with your dad and the unknowns about *ArrowVision*, or whatever it is, you stuck to the plan, and I think you helped a lot of people, Kay. I admire the hell out of you. You're incredible."

Kay pulled away and looked directly at Nick, tears welling. "Nick Knight, always the charmer." She smiled. "I couldn't have done any of this without you. Thank you." She kissed him long and hard. The safety of the kiss was a welcome relief from the insanity of the morning.

Then, from the livestream on the laptop, they heard, "Authorities have not confirmed nor denied any discoveries, but I just saw a body bag wheeled out of the investigation site." The lady news anchor reported as she stood in front of the construction site behind the Golden Sphinx.

Chapter 52

In the office at Mytherra, the BlackHole scandal was the only thing anyone could talk about. It was all over the news, flooding every screen, and coworkers gossiped about it around the coffee machine. BlackHole, the world's largest pharmaceutical corporation that seemed untouchable, was in freefall.

"They say people died. And they're saying Siren Hex knew and helped cover it up," Harold said, crunching loudly on the salt and vinegar chips Florence packed daily in his lunch.

Kay stared at the crumpled chip bag in Harold's hand, feeling guilty. She had to tell Harold about Florence's affair. But not today… *Today, enough was going on.*

He smirked, licking salt off his fingers before reaching for another chip. "Those leaked documents must be real. They just immediately went and arrested Siren at her mansion. The feds don't do that unless they have receipts." Harold nodded knowingly, as if he knew anything about how "the feds" worked. Harold was the squeakiest clean person Kay had ever met. He had never gotten so much as a parking ticket.

"Yeah, it's pretty crazy," Kay answered distantly. She was exhausted.

So, this was it? she thought to herself as Harold rambled on. *This was why I was given ArrowVision, to expose BlackHole?*

She knew that wasn't the only reason she had the power. This was just a small piece of a big puzzle. Kay knew she needed to keep using ArrowVision. And she had so much more to figure out.

She could kick back and let the ArrowVision TV play static in the back of her mind for the rest of her life, ignoring others' pain and capitalizing on the peace that came with ArrowVision, but she wasn't going to do that.

Understanding others the way she did now was a gift, and exposing BlackHole was just the beginning.

Harold finished his lunch and left the table. Kay stayed sitting a little longer by herself. She put in her headphones, and "Never Meant" by Iron & Wine played in her ears.

Kay exhaled and took a bite of her stale turkey and mustard sandwich. She leaned back in the cheap plastic breakroom chair and smiled.

For just a moment, she wanted to absorb the boringness of the breakroom and breathe a sigh of relief.

Chapter 53

5:00 p.m. – The day was a blur of gossip, headlines, and black coffee. No one got any work done at Mytherra, which was OK with Kay because she was physically and emotionally spent. She dreamed of snuggling up in her bed with Nick and Shotgun and letting sleep shut her off from the world.

Still, as she left work and walked to her Jeep, she knew there was one more thing she had to deal with today.

She pulled out her phone and started texting.

Kay: *Hey, Dad—are you home? Is it okay if I stop by real quick?*

Her phone buzzed immediately.

Bruce: *Of course, kiddo! We're here.*

Kay wondered how her family was taking the news of her grandfather, Stan, being included in the illegal BlackHole trials. Her sister, Zoey, had sent the family a text earlier that morning addressing it, and they all planned a family dinner, "just to be together," for Friday night.

The drive to the McQuinn house was hard. Kay almost turned around a dozen times. ArrowVision brought her peace, yes, but it didn't stop every bad emotion she felt. On that drive, all she felt was anxiety and sadness.

The house loomed as she pulled up the driveway, like the great protector of her parents—and her, the outcast, the unwelcome invader.

Kay entered through the garage.

"Hi, sweetie!" Pam called to her with her head down, pulling what looked like lasagna out of the oven.

Without looking up, she said, "If you're looking for your dad, I think he's in his office. This should be ready in about…"

Pam paused to examine the lasagna closely, "… fifteen minutes."

"Okay, thanks, Mom. I'll be down soon."

Kay already knew Bruce was in his office. When she pulled up, she saw his perspective through ArrowVision. He must have been upset.

Kay ascended the stairs to Bruce's office, which felt more like an evil lair.

She knocked.

"Come in!" Kay heard from the other side of the door.

Kay turned the knob.

A warm desk lamp cast a glow on Bruce's perfectly organized solid oak desk.

Atop the neat stacks of paper was an almost empty whiskey decanter; next to it was a fingerprint-smudged rocks glass.

Behind him was a built-in bookshelf stretching the length of the wall, filled with books on science, finance, leadership, and business.

Kay sat on the worn leather couch across from his desk.

Bruce looked up, the desk lamp illuminating the deep, sad lines on his face, very light streaks of gray in his black hair, and new stubble that he apparently did not care to shave. His glasses hung down at the end of his nose, and there was a familiar alcohol-induced haze over his eyes. Then Kay noticed tears. Water welled at the bottom of his eyes, ready to fall.

He looked so small. Her once towering, powerful father looked… *weak*. Had he always been like this? Or was she finally seeing him for who he was?

"Dad? Are you okay?" Kay asked as she reached out and touched his hand.

He wiped his eyes with the back of his knitted sweater sleeve.

"Oh, yeah yeah, kiddo. I'm fine. Just all this news with my company and the news of my dad—your grandfather—has me out of sorts."

Kay noted that he lamented the news about BlackHole before that of his own father.

"Yeah, the whole leak is crazy. I can't believe that Grandpa was given one of those… pills. Or something? I guess they're still trying to figure that all out."

"It's very upsetting. He was in the hospital a lot. I don't know when they could have slipped him something, or if he took something on his own, hoping it would help his heart. I don't know. I've been sitting here all day racking my brain about it. And then Siren… I knew she was bad. I knew that. But I had no idea what she was capable of. For God's sake, I was working for the company that killed my father." His words trailed off in a slight slur. More tears trickled down his cheeks.

"I'm sorry," Kay said, squeezing Bruce's hands.

Now seemed like a really crappy time to bring up her stolen art, but she had to say something.

She had concocted a cover story about how she learned about Bruce stealing her art. She definitely couldn't say, *"Oh, I think these woodland or alien beings gave me a superpower that allowed me to see through your eyes as you were texting Siren Hex."*

So instead, she said, "Hey, Dad, I know you're upset and everything. But in all the leaked documents online, I came across one today. I forget where I saw it, but it was some kind of official email. The names on the email were redacted, but it said something about 'using daughter's art for marketing.'"

She took a breath as Bruce's mopey eyes became more alert. Kay was taking a risk; she honestly didn't know if any emails existed referencing her art and her relationship with her father.

Confronting him made her feel nauseous. He was her friend, her confidant, and, in her life, the one who supported her most—besides Dee. Questioning him felt like a betrayal. Still, she knew that the true betrayal was his, not hers.

"Umm… I guess I started thinking and putting it together…"

"Yes," Bruce interrupted Kay.

He looked straight at her with his cloudy eyes, his glasses still hanging low on his nose. His voice was trembling and low. "I should have told you years ago, Kay. I suggested that BlackHole use your art. I am so sorry."

He spoke slowly, like his words would hit a mine and Kay would literally explode in front of him.

And he was right. He knew her well.

Tears started streaming down her face. She covered her eyes with her hands and sobbed into her lap. During the drive over here, she promised herself she wouldn't cry in front of him. But the betrayal stung so deeply that her heart ached. Kay was being tossed under the water that crashed after a giant wave.

Over the last several days, her life had been turned upside down. Some of what she discovered was devastating, but she hoped that the stuff about her dad wasn't true. A big part of her hoped he would deny everything.

"Mom and I were going to lose the house, Kay. Money was really tight then. I needed a great idea to keep my job. Your art is incredible. I knew people would love it. And Siren… once I mentioned it to Siren, she wouldn't let it go. Before I knew it, your art was on billboards and TV commercials— that damn Allerzil ad. I thought you'd at least get paid for it. Like, get royalties or something..."

He paused, walked around the desk, and sat down next to her on the couch.

"… I'm so sorry, kiddo. Once I knew they weren't going to pay you, I tried to help by hiring lawyers and encouraging you. I just didn't have the guts to tell you what I had done. I love you so much, and I knew you would hate me."

Kay pulled her hands from her face. Bruce's slurred speech disgusted her. She turned to him, ready to tell him off— really let him have it.

But when she looked at him, all she saw was an unhappy, tired, greedy old man. A man she loved, despite everything, so much.

All she could think to say was, "Well, at least you told me now, I guess. I'm going to need some time, Dad."

Bruce reached for her shoulder to comfort her, and she knocked his hand away.

"Don't expect to see me at dinner on Friday night."

Then she stood up, dusted herself off, and left her drunk father slouched on the couch as she slammed the office door behind her.

Chapter 54

ONE MONTH LATER

12:01 p.m. – The cabin was a mess of half-sealed boxes and random trinkets scattered around the living room. Kay had volunteered to pack up the rest of her grandmother's belongings. Dee's cabin and property had been sold to a real estate LLC. They closed on the deal a few days earlier, but the business gave the McQuinn family a grace period to remove any last-minute items from the property.

Nick insisted on helping Kay pack everything up. The McQuinn family—Bruce and his siblings—would arrive tomorrow to pick up the boxes and divvy out Dee's cherished treasures to different family members.

Kay and Nick had just finished with all the items in the kitchen cabinets and moved on to the bedroom and living room closets, which were jam-packed with odds and ends—hidden from potential buyers during showings over the last several months.

The afternoon light filtered in through the trees, warm and golden. Outside, the winter wind whispered through the pines, but inside, the only sounds were the occasional rustle of tape being pulled from the roll and John Denver quietly singing through the Bluetooth speaker in the corner.

Shotgun stood at the door, whining with a ball in his mouth, waiting for his owner to pay attention to him and play.

Kay hadn't spoken to her father since the day of the BlackHole leak. Not out of anger, necessarily—she just had nothing to say to him. She was so hurt.

Since that day, a lot had changed.

The police discovered nine bodies buried in the dirt pit behind The Golden Sphinx. It turned out that those years of construction were really a cover for using that area as a dumping ground.

From what Kay saw on the news, the authorities were still trying to piece together the purpose of the "SEE" experiments.

Kay briefly saw headlines about the Umbravue, but most got lost in the news cycle. Really, there was no public information about the Umbravue powers—only hearsay and some obscure internet forums. BlackHole had done a good job eradicating any actual Umbravue information from the internet, if there had even been any to begin with.

Jimmy, Nick's boss, stepped away from Shadowflight indefinitely and got support for his depression.

Earlier that morning, Nick had finished signing the papers to become the new owner of Shadowflight Archery. He couldn't pay for the business outright, but Jimmy and Nick negotiated a deal.

And Nick's first new hire as the owner of Shadowflight?
Kay McQuinn.

Kay quit her job at Mytherra two weeks ago. Fred was
shocked but mostly disappointed that he could no longer
take credit for Kay's work.

And Harold? Kay finally went to game night at Florence
and Harold's house before quitting her job at Mytherra.

When she had the perfect moment alone with Florence in
the kitchen, Kay, in a hushed tone, informed her that she
knew about the affair with Fred—and that if Florence
didn't tell Harold, then Kay would have to.

In the Mytherra breakroom a few days later, Harold, always
the talker and over-sharer, sadly shared with Kay that he
and Florence were separating.

The power of ArrowVision was taxing. Kay's ability to
understand and see others' perspectives—and their most
stressful moments—took a toll on her. Her goal wasn't to
meddle in lives, but to help people. She still wasn't even
sure she did that right.

ArrowVision was a TV screen, constantly playing on mute
in the back of her mind. She didn't tune in now unless she
needed to or wanted to.

She and Nick still had a lot to figure out about the
Umbravue.

A part of her knew that the ArrowVision was only the start of what she was capable of. She hadn't been able to re-create the levitating yet and hadn't quite figured out the peaceful feeling she sometimes got…

But she and Nick planned to work hard, figure out the Umbravue and Kay's powers, and buy Dee's property back as soon as possible.

Still, Kay was learning that there was beauty in enjoying life, despite the uncontrollables. *That* might have been her best accomplishment yet.

Kay let out a dramatic sigh, stretching her arms above her head.

Nick smirked, rolling his shoulders. "Want to take a break?"

Before Kay could answer, Nick pulled his phone from his pocket, tapped the screen, and set it on the couch.

Betty Who's "I Love You Always Forever" blasted through the Bluetooth speaker.

Kay let out a soft laugh. "This is what you picked?"

Nick grinned, already stepping toward her, holding out his hand. "Dance with me."

"We're in the middle of packing. All this stuff needs to be out on the porch and ready to go by the morning."

"Exactly why we should take a short dance break, Kay McQuinn," he said.

She hesitated for only a second before slipping her hand into his.

His other hand settled lightly at her waist, and hers found his shoulder. They swayed.

Kay let her head rest against his chest, feeling the rise and fall of his breath beneath her cheek. "I didn't know you danced."

"I don't," Nick admitted, his voice low. "I just figured if I did it confidently enough, you wouldn't notice."

She laughed. "Well, you're doing a terrible job of hiding it. You're stepping on my foot."

Kay tilted her head back to look at Nick, their faces inches apart.

She pressed her lips to his.

He pulled away and sang softly in her ear, "Everywhere, I will be with you… Everything I will do for you… You've got the most unbelievable blue eyes I've ever seen."

He leaned back and, with a smirk, guided her into an awkward but cute twirl.

Chapter 55

1:43 p.m. – "I'm going to grab the last few things from downstairs!" Kay shouted back to Nick as she flicked on the light over the basement stairs.

She and Nick had cleared most of the boxes from the basement, but there were a few more things to grab.

Once in the basement, Kay exhaled, running a hand through her hair as she scanned the remaining mess.

Most of the stuff was junk—old holiday decorations, cracked fishing tackle boxes, and water-stained paperbacks that no one would read again.

But then, near the back of the room, behind a leaning stack of old camping gear, something caught Kay's eye.

A large, hard-sided case.

She recognized it immediately.

Heart thudding, she crouched down and pulled the case toward herself, brushing off a thin layer of dust. The latches were stiff, but they still worked, and with a quick pop, they released.

Kay lifted the top of the case slowly, almost reverently.

There it was.

Dee's compound bow.

The cam system gleamed under the dim light, the cables still taut, the limbs carrying the same quiet power Kay remembered.

Carefully, Kay lifted it from the foam lining, feeling its weight in her hands.

Memories hit fast—the steady *thunk* of an arrow finding its target.

Her grandmother stood next to her, adjusting Kay's stance. Dee's voice was low and patient, as this bow hung in Dee's right hand.

"One red arrow can feed a whole village, Kay," Dee whispered her favorite saying.

Kay exhaled slowly as tears welled in her eyes.

Then Kay noticed small, folded pieces of paper wedged into the foam lining beneath where the bow had rested. Kay's name was scrawled on the outside of the top paper.

Kay gingerly pulled the folded papers free.

The scent of old paper and bowstring wax drifted through the air. She unfolded the lined notebook paper and began reading.

Kay

I don't know when you'll find this, but I hope it's before your thirtieth birthday. If you're reading this, then the cancer finally won, and I'm gone. I tucked this in my bow case because I've been so in and out of the hospital lately, I'm not sure when they'll keep me there for good. I know you're the only one who will open my case and take out my bow. I really intended to tell you all of this in person, but I never found the right time to do so. I'll make this as short as possible.

Our family lives on the sacred land of the Umbravue. I don't know much about them other than what I've learned over the last forty-nine years being among them and what my mother told me. The Umbravue are ancient beings. They are good. They are watchers and seers.

I know that owls are related to the Umbravue. So, if you see an owl, know that they are watching you.

I've never spoken to the creatures… exactly… but we've communicated. They do not have mouths, nor do they speak like we do. Instead, they communicate with thought and energy. They also don't eat—they're so evolved that they only feed on energy.

Sometimes they communicate through the trees or a "humming" sound, or even an owl screech.

Poor Jonny Langley was never supposed to see them that day, years ago. Normally, they are very secretive and private. Their presence can be shocking, and their powers are overwhelming to anyone who is not ready to see them. The day Jonny saw them was the day that Bruce got his powers. He was out hunting with Jonny.

I had to pay the Bennett boys a pretty penny for them to take the blame for that day and say it was all a hoax. Jonny took a little more convincing. He wouldn't let me pay him. I begged him not to share what he saw and to go along with the hoax story.

The Umbravue can gift special abilities to people they choose. They mark those people with their sacred symbol, the spiral arrow. Your father and I both have the spiral brand on our left shoulder.

For our family, traditionally, those who are chosen are the strong ones who love nature and spend the most time in it. That is why I assume that you will receive the powers.

One person from each generation of our family is gifted powers as a thank-you for tending to the land and as encouragement to "see more." The chosen person receives this gift around their thirtieth birthday.

Why their thirtieth birthday? I really don't know. Maybe they think it's a wise age. I've wondered about that.

I did the most I could with the power of sight, but I wasn't as strong or courageous as you, Kay.

I thought that when your father received powers on his thirtieth birthday, he would change the world. And, I guess, in some ways he did—but not for the better.

Your father was good. I want to believe that he still is. But when your grandfather got sick, your father became obsessed with harnessing the powers of the Umbravue. This was back when Bruce was sober and thinking clearly. That boy always, so desperately, wanted the approval of his father, Stan. So, Bruce decided that he would help—and maybe even cure—Stan.

Bruce wanted to amplify and alter the peace and spirituality component of the Umbravue powers to help your grandfather.

What Bruce never understood was that the peace part of the power only works so much. It cannot cancel out all the suffering we feel, as humans. That suffering is simply part of the human experience. We all suffer and experience darkness, Kay. The powers will not magically rid you of all your struggles, nor should it.

Your suffering helps you understand the pain in others. It connects you in a way nothing else can. Light cannot exist without dark. Seeing someone's perspective means nothing if you can't feel their pain.

Kay thought back to all the moments she had felt frustrated or anxious over the last few days, weeks, and months—despite ArrowVision. ArrowVision and the powers helped, but her darkness had never fully disappeared.

Bruce enlisted the help of Siren Hex, whom he knew from high school. Siren was a brilliant chemist and person. He also begged me to help by volunteering to test my powers, but I refused.

The power of sight from the Umbravue is a gift, Kay. It is not meant to be sold, altered, or examined.

Eventually, Bruce thought he had perfected a pill form of the Umbravue powers, with extra healing properties.

Without my knowing, and without your grandfather's consent, Bruce slipped that horrible neon-orange medicine into a drink of Stan's. Immediately, Stan went into cardiac arrest and died that same day.

I am telling you this, Kay, because I think you need to know who your father really is. I also believe that you're the only one who can stop him.

Once Stan passed away, Bruce—so far down a rabbit hole—continued experimenting with the medication. Like he had to finish what he started, no matter who he hurt.

I'm not sure of the magnitude of his crimes. Still, he's my son. I will always love him and I hope that he, too, finds peace.

Kay, I love you so much. You are strong, powerful, and good, and the Umbravue know that.

Please uncover what your father has done and stop him.

Protect our property. Bruce desperately wanted to buy it from me, but I, of course, refused. Now, I have no idea the destiny of the Umbravue land.

Remember, one red arrow can feed a whole village.

You are the red arrow, Kay. It only takes one.

Just like how one good shot can sustain a whole village, one person willing to see things differently can spread empathy and change through a whole community—and I don't know... maybe the whole world.

The spiral arrow you have seen, or will see, represents the power of one change, one shot spreading outward.

I love you,
Dee

Chapter 56

Kay sat frozen, reading the words of the letter over and over.

Memories flashed through her mind. Now that she thought about it, she never saw her grandmother or father in anything that exposed their shoulders; they always wore T-shirts or long-sleeved shirts.

Kay blinked at the letter, rubbed her eyes, and reread it. Her mind refused to process the words staring back at her. They made no sense. They couldn't. Yet, there they were, inked in sharp, undeniable strokes. Dee would never lie to her.

How could her father have the power? He was… not a superhero or a villain. *Was he?*

But Kay had used ArrowVision on her father the night of the Bicentennial. Wouldn't he have known she was using it? And Siren Hex was the true villain, wasn't she?

The room around Kay blurred. The walls stretched; the floor tilted.

"Calm down," she said aloud.

She let out a shaky breath.

Kay pressed a hand to her temple, as if that could steady the storm inside her head. Her other hand, still trembling, held the letter.

This wasn't just surprising. It was unsettling.

A million questions clawed at her, but one scratched relentlessly at her brain.

Who was Bruce McQuinn?

"Nick!" she shouted up the basement stairs in a shaky voice. "Can you come here?"

Kay didn't have a plan. She didn't know what to do or think.

Still, she knew someone who might be able to help her.

Nick came jogging down the stairs. "What's up? I just took everything in the living room out onto the porch!"

He noticed the pieces of paper sprawled on the floor and Kay's upset expression as she sat on the cold, concrete basement floor.

"Whoa," Nick said, sitting next to Kay, placing his arm around her and pulling her close. "What's going on?" he asked, concerned.

Kay looked up at him. Tears pooled at the bottom of her eyes. She blinked rapidly, trying to push them back, but the effort only made them rise faster.

She used her sleeve to dry the unwelcome tears.

Then she finally said, "We need to go visit Siren Hex."

Chapter 57

2:37 p.m. – Nick was driving.

The Bronco was barreling down the highway toward Danbury, where Siren was being held at the federal prison.

Siren Hex had been denied bail due to the magnitude of her alleged crimes and the significant resources at her disposal, which made her a high flight risk.

Kay had called about visiting hours, and Siren agreed to see her.

Kay read Dee's entire letter to Nick in the car.

She and Nick had questions. Everything kind of made sense. And then nothing made sense at all.

Dee cleared up some questions about the Umbravue but created so much doubt about Kay's father, Bruce.

The only other person who Dee implied might know about Bruce's wrongdoings was Siren Hex.

The ride was about forty-five minutes long. Kay and Nick played a game of question ping-pong—taking themselves down rabbit holes of uncertainty and possibilities.

Eventually, the Federal Correctional Institution in Danbury appeared in front of them—a scary, giant, rectangular concrete fortress surrounded by barbed wire fencing.

Nick gripped the steering wheel tighter, his eyes locked on the entrance. Then he turned to Kay. "You good?"

"Yeah. We need answers."

With that, they rolled forward to the guard at the gate.

The prison's entryway had cold tiles and scuffed, beige cinderblock walls. Fluorescent lights buzzed overhead, adding to the place's eeriness. It was a human cage. The cameras watching sent an uneasy chill up Kay's spine.

Kay was so concerned about Siren that she hadn't considered what ArrowVision would be like in a prison. That was definitely an oversight, because now she was getting a nonstop livestream in the back of her mind of anxious, angry inmate perspectives. She breathed.

The guards barely looked up as Kay and Nick passed through security; nothing more than a routine Saturday for them.

Then, Kay and Nick were escorted through a maze of hallways, all separated by heavy, auto-locking doors.

Eventually, they were led into a quieter section of the prison. The atmosphere was different here. This was the "nice" area—if such a thing exists in a place like this.

The hallway was wider; the floors, buffed to a dull shine. The air smelled faintly of industrial cleaners.

There were doors instead of bars here, with narrow windows that offered only a small view into each cell.

Finally, Kay and Nick were led into a visiting area.

A thick glass partition stretched the length of the room, dividing it cleanly down the middle.

Each station along the glass wall had the same setup: a metal counter worn smooth from years of elbows resting on it, a black phone bolted into place on each side, uncomfortable metal chairs, and the thick glass separating the visitor from the inmate they had come to see. There was no privacy, no way to lean in close.

Kay and Nick were instructed to sit at the last phone station as the guards went to get Siren Hex.

"This is kind of surreal, isn't it? Being in a place like this to visit such an important person?" Nick murmured to Kay as he looked down to adjust the chair, scooching himself closer to her and the counter.

"Super surreal," Kay agreed. Her eyes were locked on the glass in front of her. Waiting.

After a couple of minutes, Siren Hex appeared on the other side.

The guards removed her handcuffs as she sat down.

Siren was composed, as always. Prison didn't seem to affect her much.

Her dark, sleek hair was well-maintained despite the prison-issued shampoo. It was neatly parted and tucked behind her ears. Her signature bob haircut had grown to just above her shoulders.

Her skin was beautiful, even under the fluorescent lights. She somehow still held a trace of the luxury she once lived in.

Her features were sharp, her posture impeccable, her expression unreadable.

Nick's leg bounced from nerves.

Siren picked up the phone with graceful ease, her nails still manicured from whatever high-end salon she once frequented.

She put the phone to her ear, tilted her head slightly, locked her eyes onto Kay, and said, "I've been waiting for you."

Chapter 58

The phone's black plastic was cold and hard in Kay's palm. The subtle phone frequency buzzed in her ear.

"What do you mean?" Kay asked Siren.

Siren had a motherly softness in her eyes, almost like she pitied Kay.

"I wasn't sure how long it would take you both to figure out that I am not the villain in this story."

"I mean… I'm not sure about that. It's your signature on all those death certificates the authorities found."
Kay shot back, but really, she wasn't sure she believed Siren was evil, either.

For a moment, a look of pain flashed across Siren's face.

She winced at the words *death certificate.*

Then she regained her composure and, now visibly irritated, asked, "Then why are you here, Kay?"

Now, that was a hard question to answer… *Because my grandma left me a letter claiming that some owl creature gave my dad a superpower, and now he is a monster, and maybe only you know all the evil shit he has done.*

Instead, Kay blurted out, "Was my dad part of the 'SEE' project?"

"Kay, I think you know the answer to that question. But I'll tell you anything you need to know," Siren responded.

Kay sat up straighter. This was it—even if she didn't want to know the truth: "Did my father ask you to help him create the pill that I read about in the leaked 'SEE' file?"

"Yes," Siren affirmed. There was sadness in her voice.

Nick sat calmly next to Kay, observing, his hand on her knee for support.

Siren continued, "I tipped you off about the 'SEE' file. I am MrStrange_8937."

Now Kay was surprised. "Wait, that makes no sense. Why would you get yourself arrested?"

Siren sighed. She was a defeated woman.

"For a year or so now, I've been trying to leak information about BlackHole, 'SEE,' or the Umbravue on the internet, but Bruce has the best internet scrubbers working to remove all information, all the time."

"Kay, your father… is a complicated guy… I think he used to be good. That's how I remember him, anyway, when he first came to me to tell me about the Umbravue and his powers."

Siren repositioned herself in her chair.

"Your grandfather, Stan, was sick. Bruce was already working for BlackHole. He was one of our smartest, brightest employees. Bruce approached me one day, in secret, and explained that he might have a cure-all for illnesses. He said that, with my help, we could create a pill that, at the very least, would put people at peace and make them comfortable. But he was convinced that if we worked on the formula together, we could alter and amplify Umbravue powers and make a pill that cured any illness."

She paused.

"Of course, this sounded far-fetched to me. But once Bruce showed me his power of sight, his levitating, the information about the Umbravue, your grandmother's land, and other discoveries he had made, I was convinced we could create the pill. One medication to *maybe* solve everything. We wanted to take the powers of the Umbravue and study them—*modify* them."

Kay and Nick just stared in shock, unsure of what to say.

"Bruce was obsessed with healing his father. He loved him so much. And I was obsessed with success. Plus, after losing my husband, a cure-all medication sounded like a dream. Together, we started testing. Bruce, of course, had to test on himself since, besides your grandmother, he was the only one with Umbravue powers. At that point, we hadn't hurt anyone. We just spent a lot of time in the lab running tests and gathering as much knowledge about the Umbravue as possible. All in secret, of course."

Siren took a moment to fix her hair. She spoke
condescendingly, as if she weren't the one behind bars.

"Then your grandfather got *really* sick. Without my
knowing, Bruce decided to slip Stan the pill before the pill
was ready—before we figured out the healing potential or
side effects. Bruce claimed slipping his father the pill was
the only choice. Well, the pill sent your grandfather into
cardiac arrest."

"Your father killed his dad—your grandfather, Kay." Siren
paused. Her voice was soft.

Kay didn't know what to say. Nick squeezed her leg.
Before she could speak, Siren continued.

This was a confession.

"After that, Bruce started drinking again. He barely slept.
He was constantly buried under books, papers, and to-go
coffee cups, trying to amplify the Umbravue powers in pill
form. He wasn't just obsessed—he was completely
consumed. Bruce kept testing on himself, using his own
blood, to perfect the pill. I begged him to stop. That's when
he started threatening me. He needed my company,
BlackHole—my resources, and my skill set. So he began
using his power of sight to manipulate everyone and
everything around him."

"At first, when he threatened to kill my daughter, I thought
it was a hollow, alcoholic ramble. But then he began testing
the pill on human subjects. He mostly found degenerate
people around The Golden Sphinx who had no connection

to family. People society wouldn't miss. Bruce would pay them to take the pill. Desperate for money, they would take it willingly, not knowing they were signing their own death certificate."

Kay's mind flashed to seeing Siren near The Golden Sphinx days earlier—and to the list of deaths in the 'SEE' file.

"What about Marcus Knight and Penny Grant?" Kay asked.

"Well, Bruce got drunker and drunker and sloppier and sloppier. Some pills leaked out to parties—hence Penny's death. Marcus Knight suspected something was happening, and Bruce slipped him a pill to stop him from investigating."

Nick put his head in his hands and mumbled a muffled, "What the fuck?"

Siren didn't acknowledge him. She continued, like she had been waiting years to get all this off her chest.

"Once Bruce was killing people, I knew his threats weren't empty. He threatened me all the time. That's why I resorted to trying to leak information online. Then you two came along. It was perfect because I knew you could steal your dad's keycard to get into BlackHole."

Kay was frustrated now. "Hang on, hang on." She leaned in.

"Then why did you steal my art, and how did I use my power on my dad the other night if he is, like, 'all-knowing' and 'so evil'?"

Siren looked visibly shocked. "I didn't steal your art!"

"Sure you did. I saw him texting you the other night at the Bicentennial. You've seen the Allerzil ads—you know that's my art. I fought BlackHole in court about it."

Siren didn't skip a beat.

"Don't you get it, Kay? Bruce knows you have the power. He was manipulating you and acting anxious so that you would see his perspective. I never even received a text. So, he must not have sent it. He wanted you to believe that *I* was the bad guy."

Siren rolled her eyes and threw her hands in the air. "*This* is what he does! He manipulates." She said it like she was talking about an annoying toddler.

"Kay, I need you to hear me and believe me. Your father stole your art. He approached BlackHole with the art as if it were his own. Then he altered it a bit to, in his words, 'help it fit the Allerzil ad campaign better.' None of us knew it was your art until the campaign went live. Then Bruce worked with our legal team to bury your career. Sure, I knew he hired an attorney for you, but behind the scenes, he was pulling the strings to have our legal team ruin you."

Now Kay was furious. "Why would *my own dad* do that?!"

"Because he needed you back in Owlsbourne, Kay. He knew that you'd go right to your grandmother's property and, as a result, eventually be gifted powers by the Umbravue. He needed you here to run tests on you and study you. Bruce can't test himself anymore, or he will die. That's why he looks so terrible."

Kay thought about her father's appearance and how she had attributed it to him drinking again.

Siren could tell what Kay was thinking. "Why do you think he looks so *horrible* lately, Kay? He is dying. Between the drinking and the tests, he has destroyed his body."

"He is convinced that he's just about to have a 'breakthrough'"—Siren put *breakthrough* in quotes—"and develop the greatest medication humanity has ever seen. He needed you to have powers, and he needed to test you. So he manipulated your whole life and ruined your career so that you would return to Owlsbourne."

"Why didn't he just tell me all of this and ask for my help?" Kay spat at Siren.

"Because your dad loves you, Kay. As fucked up as that sounds. He claimed he would tell you everything when you got back to Owlsbourne. But then, he was always making excuses that he couldn't find the right time to tell you. I think, deep down, he was afraid he might kill you if he started running tests and things went wrong." Siren sighed, annoyed.

"Two more minutes," the guard shouted from the other side of the room.

"So, if you feel so guilty, why didn't you do the right thing and tell the police about everything?" Kay accused.

Siren sat in silence. Then, softly, she answered, "I think I'm a monster, too."

She continued, "But I needed to protect my daughter from Bruce—just in case. Now she is in a safe place. A place that I planned for her to go. And I was able to leak the 'SEE' file without your father knowing it was me. I'm sure he was relieved to have me take the blame."

The three of them sat in silence, staring at each other. Kay and Nick were in shock. Siren, on the other hand, looked unbothered—relieved, even—as if she had just confessed all her sins and was waiting for her easy penance of five Hail Marys to absolve all her wrongdoings.

Then the guard walked across the room, handcuffs out. "Alright, time's up."

That wasn't enough time. Kay needed more answers.

"Wait, no. Can we have just a few more minutes?" Kay pleaded through the glass to the guard.

"Sorry, no can do. That's the rules," the guard answered, not looking up, as she secured the handcuffs onto Siren's wrists.

Siren turned back to Kay before being marched through the auto-locking door.

"Kay, I wish I had done things differently. I do. But I didn't. Please stop your father before it's too late."

Then the guard gently pushed Siren through the open door, back toward the cellblock.

Chapter 59

Kay and Nick were escorted out of the building.

Once back in the Bronco, they sat silently for a few moments, processing.

"So, my dad killed your dad?" Kay finally said, meekly, addressing the elephant in the room.

"I mean… I guess?" Nick responded as he stared blankly forward, lost in thought.

Kay, more alert now: "I mean, I don't know if Siren is telling the truth. Regardless, she is a murderer and a criminal. She could just be passing the blame…" Kay paused.

"But still, *a lot* of it makes sense. I don't know how Siren could know all of that and not be at least somewhat telling the truth."

Nick sat on the driver's side, frozen. He was rattled; Kay could tell. Kay was rattled too, but at this point, she wanted to solve everything.

She didn't dare move closer or touch Nick. Kay was embarrassed. She was embarrassed about her drunk (maybe murderer) father, her career, her financial situation, that she ever pulled Nick into all of this, and how she handled… life in general.

Nick had been so kind and stoic and impossibly stable through everything, and now he had to confront his father's death all over again—all because of Kay and her greedy family.

"I'm sorry," was all Kay could think to say.

"I'm just really sorry, Nick."

He sat there for another moment, then turned to Kay. Nick looked her in the eyes.

"Kay, never apologize to me for something out of your control. If Siren is right, this is your father's mess, not yours," he said as he took her hand.

"I'm upset, yes. But you are remarkable. I have only seen you take these powers and do incredible things with them. You amaze me. Now you just found out that your dad possibly killed your grandfather, your best friend, a bunch of other people, and ruined your career—and you're sitting here apologizing to me. Don't. Let's get to the bottom of this. I'm here with you, and I'm not going anywhere."

Kay stared at him. His face was so beautiful and genuine. His brown eyes were soft and held so much sadness.

"Okay, let's do it, then," Kay agreed as she held his hand.

Nick nodded and said, "I think I know exactly where we need to go."

He let go of her hand and turned the key in the ignition.

Chapter 60

5:53 p.m. – The night felt black and suffocating. An owl flew overhead as they turned onto the McQuinns' street.

Kay had no idea what she would say to her dad. She just knew that she had to confront him again.

Her stomach turned. Even if he had done all these terrible things, he was still her father. A part of her still respected and feared him. To walk into his house and accuse him of so much evil felt wrong.

A part of Kay still wanted him to be the person she thought he was—the person she saw as a little girl—her rock, strong and protective.

Nick pulled up the driveway. The house loomed above them, threatening.

Nick parked the truck. The engine's hum died, leaving only the sound of the wind threading through the perfectly trimmed trees that lined the driveway.

"Ready?" Nick asked.

"No," Kay answered, staring at the house.

"Want me to come in with you?"

"Thank you, but no. This is something I need to do on my own. I need answers from my dad."

Nick leaned in, grabbed Kay's face, and turned it toward his.

"You got this. I love you." Then he kissed her lips.

She wanted to enjoy the moment, but all she could think about was what awaited her.

"I love you. Here I go," Kay said, reaching over to pull the handle to open the passenger door.

Kay entered the house through the garage, like she always did.

Inside, her mom wasn't buzzing around as usual. Kay would have texted beforehand to ensure her parents were home, but she thought a text might spook him—if her dad was as bad as Siren described.

"Mom! Dad!" Kay yelled up the stairs.

Nothing. No response.

Then Luke, Kay's brother, wandered up from the finished basement. His hair was a mess; he had clearly been sleeping. He was groggily scrolling through Streamo (a social media app for viral dance videos) on his phone.

He didn't look up as he walked past Kay. "Kay, what are you doing here? You woke me up." He sounded annoyed as he led himself to the pantry and started rummaging for a snack, viral videos still looping on his phone.

"Where are Mom and Dad?" Kay asked.

Luke was buried in the pantry now.

"I thought Mom just bought more granola bars, but I can't find them." His phone was now resting on a neighboring shelf, still playing some viral audio clip over and over.

"Luke! Where are Mom and Dad?" Kay was very frustrated now.

He turned to finally look at her, his eyes slits from the weed he'd smoked earlier.

"Jeez, chill out. They went on a trip or something. They said they'd be back in a few days… or a week… or something." He went back to rummaging as his phone played the same video again.

"What? Where did they go? When did they leave?" Kay was yelling now.

"Calm down, sis. I don't know. They left a few days ago. I don't remember where they were going… or maybe they didn't tell me…" Luke paused, lost in uncertainty.

"Okay, thanks," Kay said flatly, then turned and walked out of the house and back to the Bronco.

"That was quick," Nick said, confused, as Kay climbed into the passenger seat, visibly flustered.

"They weren't home. My stupid brother said they left on a trip, but he doesn't know where they went or how long they'll be gone."

"Oh," Nick said, thinking. "That's weird. Do you think your dad knows you visited Siren?"

"I don't kn—"

Before Kay could finish her sentence, her brain was sucked into someone else's perspective.

ArrowVision ran passively in the back of Kay's mind. She could tune in when she wanted to, but not this time.

She had no control, as if her mind was commanded to tune in to ArrowVision.

She was seeing through her father's eyes, which she knew meant he had to be close.

His familiar, scarred right hand was texting a message on a burner flip phone.

Kay watched as the letters formed four words across the phone screen:

Grandma's. Midnight. Alone. Dad.

Then the hands flipped the phone shut, and Kay was back in the Bronco, sitting next to Nick.

Chapter 61

11:57 p.m. – They arrived at the cabin just before midnight. Nick stopped the Bronco a few feet from the porch. "Want me to come with you?"

Kay shook her head. "No. I need to see him alone."

She stepped out and approached the front door. Her boots crunched through the frostbitten leaves.

The front door was ajar. A faint light glowed inside.

She hesitated. Her heartbeat was slow and heavy.

Kay pushed it open. The hinges groaned. Then, she stepped in.

The fireplace was lit. Bruce was sitting at the kitchen table toward the back of the cabin.

He didn't look up at first. He was hunched slightly, his elbows on the table, his hands clasped in front of him.

Kay stepped farther into the cabin, and the door swung shut behind her.

As she moved into the firelight, something caught her eye—just beneath the fabric of Bruce's white T-shirt, faint but unmistakable, was a neon-orange spiral arrow glowing in the center of his chest.

It pulsed.

She stared.

Kay didn't speak again. She just looked at him, waiting.

"Hey, kiddo," he said softly.

She didn't answer right away. She studied him, searching for the man she remembered.

"Is it true?" she asked finally. Her voice cracked. "The testing… the pill… Penny. Grandpa."

Bruce closed his eyes and exhaled.

"I need to explain," he said quietly. "You only know parts of the story…"

Outside, there was the distant hoot of an owl.

Then the woods went silent.